Sexaholics Anonymous: Road To Recovery

*To my inspiration, my muse, thank you for motivating me but also telling me to breathe when I became overwhelmed.
Thank you so much, my love.*

There's always something or someone blocking you from trying to do the best you can. You tell them about your improvements and they consistently bring up your past. You have to remind them, that's not who you are anymore. You want better for yourself. But forget about proving that to anyone else.

Dr. Johnson has been pushing for me to know my worth. To understand that I do not need sex to feel good about myself. That everything I am doing with multiple men, can be saved for one. He's also teaching me about self love, that my body is my temple and I need to protect it. Dr. Johnson lets me know I can't keep allowing demons to enter my body. With every situation that I opened up about, he helped me find solutions. I wasn't sure if I'm ready to leave the facility but I can't stay in hiding forever. I have learned self control.

After three months living in rehab, I'm taking the steps of leaving Dr. Johnson behind. Walking out those doors entering my new life. I'm thankful for all I learned and glad my friends on the outside didn't talk me out doing this for myself. I hugged Dr. Johnson then walked away without looking behind. Something about turning around makes me feel like I'm already looking back into my past. But as I got in my car, I took one look into the rearview mirror and had a slight fear of returning. This road to recovery is definitely going to an obstacle course.

What if I become overly horny? Or seduce a man into fucking me? Or if someone shows interest and I don't know what to do? I'm not relationship material, hell I don't even know how to be in a relationship. My thing is a quick fling and then it's over. Maybe I shouldn't leave the facility just yet. I feel my anxiety starting to flare and become nervous. As I'm trying to calm myself down, a knock on my window makes me jump. I look over to see Dr. Johnson. I roll my window down and before I ask what's going on, he instantly says, "Drive. It's okay to be scared but you have my number and email if you need to reach out. Just because you are leaving rehab, doesn't mean I'm leaving you completely alone. But you'll be okay Nomi.".

I decided to breathe and take his words to heart, and drive. It's time to make this change. It's time for the next step in life. Let's see what going through recovery is like.

The last six months have been interesting. I only focus on work and go home. If I choose to step out and enjoy a self care day, I'll do everything early so I won't have to interact with anyone. It's as if my social anxiety heightened because I'm scared to turn back into a nympho. Seeing an attractive man, not sure how I'll react. One thing that really drives me insane is my messages. I've had men that I've ignored in the past, reach out to me hoping for a chance. Sometimes I wonder what if I didn't give you a chance during my hoe phase, why would I give you a chance now? Then it hit me. I don't have to have sex with these men. Intimacy comes in many different forms. Maybe the next message I receive, I'll put myself back out there. Test myself and see if I have control.

Over the next few days, my phone has stayed dry. Why when I decide to welcome the male species back in my life, it becomes crickets? My best friend, Michelle, came bursting into my room yelling, "Your 30th birthday in a few days!!". I've been so isolated from the world trying to get my life back on track, I didn't realize my birthday was around the corner. After I left rehab, Michelle let me move in with her so she can watch over me to make sure I don't "relapse". But I kept myself busy. She just sent texts if she cooked or wanted to chill to catch up on the latest tea. One thing Michelle was going to do is drag me out the house to go celebrate. Maybe this is what I need. Time to get my feet wet a little bit. "So what are we doing for your day because

we're not sitting in the house. I was thinking of throwing you a party, or going to karaoke or bar hop."

I decided on both karaoke and some bar hopping. We contacted a few friends and got a plan together. And being a summer baby, everyone wanted to make sure I made the plans at night. As I was out having a pre birthday lunch to celebrate myself, I felt a weight lifted off my shoulders. Nine months ago I was walking myself into a sex rehabilitation center. Spent three months getting my mind, body, and soul back in order. Some people couldn't understand and thought I was being dramatic about my sex life. I kept that part of my life private, so of course they wouldn't understand that I had a football team of men on me for one month from time to time. How I had sex with two men in one day, hours apart from one another. I looked for satisfaction in many different forms. It was a different craving from each man. I'm not saying that being out of rehab life is great and all. I'm too busy living in fear. I have to come back to reality.

While sitting at the bar at my favorite sushi restaurant, I look to the side of me and can't help but notice this attractive man. I couldn't stop staring at him. While he was taking his order, his pearly white teeth stood out to me. His light brown eyes are hypnotizing, the dimple at the crease of his lips when he smiles is mesmerizing, and the sight of his muscular broad shoulders is melting my insides. Before I got a chance to look away, our eyes matched and he smiled and I turned away.

When the bartender returned to me and asked if I wanted another drink, I responded, "Why not, you only turn thirty once!". The bartender told me happy birthday and looked over at the attractive man and told him to come over and take a shot. Shots on the house for me. I felt special and of course when asked my type of liquor to take a shot of, tequila me please.

As I was getting ready to pay, my bartender said it's on the house. I smiled and thanked him. The attractive man approached me. "Hello beautiful, I couldn't let you leave without at least getting your name. Happy birthday also. My name is

Jabari.". Now this is the test. Am I comfortable enough to introduce myself? Come on Nomi, calm yourself down. It's a small and brief introduction. No one said I have to fuck the man. May not even talk to him after today anyway. "My name is Nomi, and thank you for taking a birthday shot with me." Looking at Jabari with that beautiful smile of his gave me butterflies but in my pussy. It's been a long time since I've been touched by a man and even talked to one. Something about him has me ready to risk it all. I can't explain it, but I'm usually the one that approaches someone that I want to spend a little time with.

"Nomi, can I take you out for a birthday dinner? Or just in general? I would love to get to know you and potentially pursue you.". I didn't know how to respond. How and why is he coming so forward. So blunt. It's actually turning me on. If Jabari knew that I don't even date, I wonder how he'll react. Shit, I can't even remember my last date. I think this is my chance to be open. It's only a date. But he said pursue me too. Fuck it. I accepted Jabari's date and gave him my number. I walked out of the restaurant feeling a little excited yet nervous.

Getting back home, I walked into lots of screams and balloons everywhere. A few friends stopped by to surprise me for my birthday. Turning thirty is a milestone that I am glad I get to celebrate. I found Michelle in the cloud of balloons and pulled her to the side. I let her know about my lunch earlier and how I might have a date if Jabari actually falls through with his word. "Wait a fuckin' minute! You step out for lunch like you normally do and on your birthday, God says here is this man. Go into your thirtieth birthday with a man?! I'm actually glad you decided to give it a chance. I was worried about you. Thought you were swearing off all types of intimacy." Michelle said.

    I know my girl means no harm but I had to let her know I had to get back in tune with myself. Michelle is the main one that knows all that I was doing. She knew I took YOLO to another level. I was living life on the edge, sexually. That part of me wanted to find excitement in my boring life. Thinking about it, it wasn't all bad but I didn't know how to stop. Reasons why rehab played a part in my decision to stop.

    As my friends were pregaming before stepping out to karaoke, I decided I'll go get ready. I wanted to be sexy but comfortable. Comfort will always follow me in anything I wear. Red tank top, black ripped shorts, flannel tied around the waist, with high top all white platform converse. I put my braids in a high bun. Finished off with a red lipstick and sprayed Versace Bright Crystal for the finishing touch. Walking out my room, coming down the stairs, each friend stood on the stairs holding a shot. That's how they wanna play?! Michelle explained that I'm too sober and we need to be lit for karaoke. Six friends, six shots. Back to back. Even had Drake's Back to Back playing.

I'm honestly thankful for my girls. In rehab, each one came to visit me. Renee always gave me the latest tea. Chloe gave me books to read. Lowkey felt like I was truly locked up with her doing that. Tiana kept me fed. Ashley snuck wine in and we would knock out afterwards. My forever nap friend. Nala would bring my Goddaughter Zuri to come see me and we would have a blast until Zuri was knocked out. And of course Michelle came even when she wasn't supposed to. We had set visitor days and she would pull up and come to the fence and we would talk that way. The security guard got tired of trying to chase her away so he left us alone. Each one had a piece of my heart and I don't know what I would have done without them.

When I got to the bottom of the stairs, I almost cried. Zuri was holding a capri sun for me. "Here you go NoNo. Mommy said you will need this.". Everyone laughed and I picked Zuri up to give her a hug. No matter how down I get or too far in my thoughts I'm lost, Zuri will always remind me that her NoNo needs her. My goddaughter has struggled to say Nomi, and NoNo just stuck with me. Even with her being four years old, she finally got my name down but I wouldn't allow it. I love the nickname she has for me. While we waited for Nala's husband, Elijah, to come pick up Zuri, we made TikToks and played games. "Mommy I'm sleepy." Zuri said as she's getting off her mom's lap to come sit on my lap to lay on me. Nala loved our bond but whenever Zuri started acting up she would call me to come get her. I felt my tipsy self getting tired and I couldn't be more excited when I heard Elijah was outside. My baby girl was heading home and we were heading out!

On the way to karaoke, I received a text from Jabari. And the pursuing begins.

Maybe: Jabari
Hey beautiful, I hope you're enjoying your birthday and wanted to see about taking you on a date, Monday night at seven. It's Jabari.

Right to the point. My kind of guy. I let him know that Monday night and that time works for me. As I looked up from my phone, all eyes were on me. They started questioning me right away and

Michelle busted out laughing. I told them all about my lunch earlier, and how Jabari approached me. Within five minutes of the conversation, Renee had all his socials pulled up. Each one gave compliments and agreed he is very attractive. Renee is who we like to consider the private investigator of the group. "Girl, he ain't from here! But all the hoes follow him. Now we gotta make sure he ain't run through them." Renee said. I let her know it's just a date. Nothing serious. I just met the guy, no need to get all worked up on.

We pulled up to karaoke and before we got out, we took some more shots before heading in. The girls made me go in last which was a dead giveaway that it's a party inside for me. But then it could be to make me feel special as they hold the doors for me. As I'm walking up the steps Nala and Chloe are each holding a door. When I got inside, I was smiling ear to ear. From family to friends was here to celebrate with me. I knew with my time away and not letting people know where I was, I felt many would cut me off. But this crowd definitely reads, "we all have a life and life be lifin' but we are always going to show up for one another.".

I saw a few of my guy friends and went right to them. Douglas was the best male friend I have. He actually told me to stop being a pussy and don't go to rehab. Douglas felt that rehab can't help me. "Sex is something people do. Either you do or you don't. You do it a lot or you do it very little. But don't beat yourself up for something that is pleasurable and enjoyable to you.". That was the last thing he said before I told him how bad I was. It was at that moment Douglas understood but still told me I could find self control on my own. Seeing Douglas at my party made me happy because he knew how to have fun and didn't care how people viewed him. When I saw my other guy friend I'm close with, I walked up to him and punched him on his arm. Lawrence turned around and gave me a bear hug. Right when he let go, he said he wanted to introduce me to his cousin who just moved here a few months ago. Here goes Lawrence being a matchmaker. As I'm following behind Lawrence, I notice a new familiar face. "Jabari?!". Lawrence looked confused and asked how I knew his cousin.

"I met this birthday queen today at lunch, and already asked her out. I beat you to it Lawrence, but glad you know my taste in beautiful women" Jabari said while staring into my eyes. Damn, why is he looking at me like this? He's waking up my Pandora box and I wonder if he knows it. The feeling of my wetness had me wanting to sit on his dick. The image of me riding him while he sucks on my nipples kept playing in my head. I had no clue what Jabari and Lawrence was talking about because I kept thinking about getting fucked. Do I even want Jabari to touch me? His energy is strong and him having my mind run wild is having me second guess him.

Michelle caught me in thought and told me my cat is purring at me. I really hate that she knows me at times. I know me biting my lip was a dead giveaway. I need to control myself. She only laughed at me and told me the girls were putting in songs to sing and I need to add one to the list. While everyone mingling and taking shots the beat drops for Juvenile Slow Motion and I notice one of the guys up on the stage with a mic. How is the night about to go? Jabari walks up to me while I'm talking to Nala and tells me to get to the dance floor. I couldn't resist. Everyone was already singing along and dancing. Jabari gave me space to dance but I pulled him in closer. Let's say it was liquid courage. I started to grind on him and decided to be a little extra and bounce this ass up and down to get a feel. The blood is definitely flowing through his dick because this man is soft but that length is there.

"Damn Nomi, tell me this your song without telling me this is your song?!" as he is grabbing at my waist to grind with me. The closer Jabari is pulling me in, the more I feel weak. It's been almost a year since I've been touched, including me not even touching myself. But I can't touch myself or it will make me crave for some dick. Yes it's about having self control but that is one thing I have no self control over. Something about pleasuring myself unleashes all the horniness inside of me and I will have to fuck someone.

That little black book of names, someone will get a call. Something in me said to slow down. I felt a rush come over me, almost forgetting all my progress in the past months. Instantly I went into panic mode. What kind of voodoo did Jabari have on me? I had to control myself but inside, I wanted to run. Once the song was over, I broke free. I let him know I was going to find my girls.

Chloe is my spiritual friend. She looks deep into things and I feel like she'll understand me. "So Jabari is pulling me in pretty fast and it's like all my progress and working on myself is going out the window. I've been approached by men since I've been out of rehab but it's different this time. All I can think about is dick and fucking and dick some more. His energy is welcoming in a sexual way." Chloe couldn't do anything but laugh. She said that it's probably me being horny but does agree that his energy is overly welcoming. The fact Chloe also felt it by being in his presence gave me a little clarity that I'm not completely crazy.

Part of me was ready to crawl back into bed and wish I didn't decide to force myself to test the waters. As I was about to tell my girls I'm ready to go back home, the DJ called my name to sing next. There's no way I'm getting out of this. Renee walked up with two shots and I snatched both and took them back to back. "Damn girl, nervous to sing?!" said Renee. I'm not nervous about singing, I just needed more liquid courage. I walked up to the mic and waited for the lyrics to appear.

Once the crowd saw "I wanna sex you" appear they went crazy. Love like Honey by Pretty Ricky is my go to. Once I started singing, it's like the liquor kicked in and I didn't care how I sounded. Jabari started coming towards me and I grabbed Michelle and we started singing and dancing together. Once I was done singing, the table where we were sitting was full of food. Just what I needed. With all the drinking, some salt and pepper chicken wings with rice and sauteed onions does me right every time.

The bar hopping didn't happen, it never does. Whenever karaoke is involved, the night ends there. While walking to the car with my girls, Jabari and Lawrence came up to us to say goodbye. Jabari made it a public announcement to say he will see me Monday night for our date. Of course the girls had a field day with that. Nala being the mom friend is overprotective of us. She kept getting bad vibes when being around Jabari and she didn't know why. I told her it's just a date. Why do I feel like I have to keep saying it's just a date? This is my first time stepping out and it feels like everyone is concerned. Do I have to remind them that I don't date? That can actually be why they're concerned. I was the meet, fuck, and on to the next type. I had a rotation. So now that someone wants to take me on a date and I'm for it, shouldn't they see that as growth? I want to try and meet someone's mind instead of their dick. It's all new to me.

Once we got back to the house, everyone said their last happy birthdays to me and then went to sleep. Getting in bed, I started thinking maybe thirty will be good for me. It had a good start and ending. Celebrated with people I love. Have a date in a couple days. I decided to try not living in fear. Life is going to keep going so why should I stay on pause? There's more to life I want for myself and I am going to go after it. Claim it all.

After a hard weekend of turning up for my birthday, I was excited that I took Monday off from work. It felt like my soul left my body and the bed was the only place I wanted to be. Michelle knocked and came into my room announcing that my date is tonight. FUCK! Been drinking so much and having fun it slipped my mind. When I reached for my phone, I had a text from Jabari reminding me of our date. Well at least he is staying on top of it while I'm slacking. He also mentioned that he's taking me to Morton's Steakhouse. There goes my somewhat comfortable wardrobe. I showed Michelle the text and she got excited. Two things Michelle loves to do is make-up and pick out outfits. Before I had a chance to respond to Jabari, he sent another text asking if he could pick me up. Michelle snatched my phone and replied yes because she knew I was going to say no. I rolled my eyes and told Michelle to give me an hour to calm my nerves before she starts making me get ready.

Why would Jabari pick a steakhouse for our first date? I don't even care for steak. But it's not even about that, dressing up takes so much effort and time and I want to look my best. I closed my eyes to get a vision of my outfit and everything is falling into place in my mind. Black dress of course, gold accessories is a must, and shoes are the struggle. I can see it now, Michelle giving me a pair of her heels to wear. In the middle of thinking about what I'm wearing, I feel myself drifting into a nap and I was not planning on stopping this sleep. I don't know how long I checked out from reality but woke up to Michelle yelling it's time to get that ass up.

While sitting up in bed, I started to think about my dream. I had a sex dream and it was fuckin amazing. I couldn't see the face, but the hands pleasuring my body made me quiver just at the thought of it. Then the tongue motion had me wishing it was really done to me. This man in my dreams was licking everywhere on me. Started off by sucking on my bottom lip, then moved to my neck, making his way to my breast only to start sucking and licking on the side of my titty before taking my nipple in his mouth. While sucking on my nipple, he takes his other hand and begins to play with my pussy. As he is doing that, he stops sucking on my nipple and begins kissing down my body before spreading my lips and taking my clit in his mouth, licking it in circular motion. When he started sucking on my clit, I woke up.

Thinking about that dream, playing it over in my head had me reach down in between my legs to feel my pussy. I'm already dripping. As I start to reach to insert two fingers inside of me, Michelle knocks on the door, causing me to jump. I told her to come in. She opens the door with outfits and heels and her makeup bag. When I reached to touch my head, I realized the girls and I took my braids out last night while drunk because I was complaining about them needing to be redone.

"Michelle!!! I have to figure out what to do with this mess on my head!"

Michelle told me to get in the shower so we can tackle my hair right away. I reminded her to leave the straightener away from my head. It's hot out and I'll just rock my curls. In the shower, I started thinking about Jabari. The amount of sexual thoughts this man has brought into my life since

I've been out of rehab, doesn't make any sense. How do you meet someone for a day, and your pussy won't stop being wet? I've been as dry as the sahara desert and now I'm awake and ready to fuck. I start to wash my body and when I get to my titties, I wash around my nipples until they get hard. I squeeze my nipples and right as I feel a moan coming, BANG BANG BANG! Michelle knocked on the door for me to hurry up. This girl is gonna make me move out if she keeps interrupting my time with sensual thoughts.

Once I was done in the shower, I grabbed my curl cream and started to part my hair to do bantu knots. Michelle was sitting on my bed when I opened the bathroom door, with a black strapless maxi dress and gold sandals and gold accessories. I'm glad the footwear is something I can work with because I'm not feeling heels. While Michelle starts to work on my makeup, the first thing she said to me is to go ahead and fuck him. "Nomi, remember when I used to tell you that you moan in your sleep? That has happened every night since you met Jabari. He clearly has woken up the sex demon inside of you. You've been doing great since you left rehab. No one is saying start back your starting team, but one person is not going to mess up your progress. Just think about it."

First off, I'm not even shocked I'm back to moaning in my sleep. But it's something about Jabari that I can't put my finger on. He's taking over my body. I welcomed him in with one dance and now feel like he put a spell on me that I need to figure out how to break.

My makeup was done, took my bantu knots out to let my spiral curls bounce with laid edges. Slipped on the dress and now I see why Michelle picked this dress. It hugs my ass perfectly. After putting on my accessories, I finished off with a light floral scent, Gucci Bloom. Looking at myself in the mirror is making me want to cancel and get back in bed. I have to remind myself it's okay to date, let a man show off all this beauty. Nothing is wrong with dinner. The bedroom isn't the only place my mouth opens. I had to laugh at myself thinking that. Why am I so nasty? While I continued to stare at myself, Michelle picked out a lipstick for me to wear but I wanted my lips to just be a clear gloss. She was about to talk me out of it until my phone vibrated and we both looked down at it. Michelle grabbed my phone and said Jabari is at the door, that he's been knocking. She ran out to open it and made me wait before coming downstairs.

I came out of my room and heard Jabari and Michelle laughing. I'm not ready to face him but he's here and I'm going to get his night over with. I tried to come down the stairs quietly but Michelle walked over and said, "here she comes". When Jabari stepped to the stairs, and the way this man was dressed, had me ready to suck his dick. Who the fuck goes on a date in a suit?! All black suit and some Stacy Adams?! Now I want to at least change into heels because who told this man to step out like this. His shirt under the jacket was opened up showing his chest with a gold chain. The fresh line up with the waves is definitely making me seasick. I gave Michelle an evil glare because she should've sent a text letting me know what he was wearing. She caught the glare and turned away.

"You look really beautiful Nomi."

The butterflies in my stomach are going crazy and I don't know how to calm them down. Hearing Jabari compliment me, brings the girly girl out of me and I get all giggly. When I got in front of him, he hugged me and I took in his scent. No clue what he is wearing but it has me wanting to give him a kiss on his neck. As he walks me to the door to head out, Michelle yells out don't do anything she wouldn't do. Jabari laughed at her and winked saying, "With Nomi wearing this dress, and its hugging in all the right areas, I can't make any promises". My face lights up and I can't do anything but laugh nervously. I know my thoughts of being fucked by him has my mind running wild but I'm sure he was just joking about that statement.

    Jabari opens the door for me and right when he shuts it, I text the group chat that I'm on the date and to watch my location. I put my phone on do not disturb and back in my purse it goes. On the drive to the restaurant, Jabari and I had good conversations. Of course I had to ask what made him move to Portland. He told me he needed a change of scenery. Seeing the same faces, doing the same things. Jabari moved to Portland from Las Vegas. All the partying, gambling, and fucking got the best of him. He wanted something more quiet and out of the way. Jabari explained that seeing Lawrence thrive and succeed with all his accomplishments, made him want to step up and better his life. It is true, Lawrence is doing great for himself. He's a thirty-four year old college football coach and just purchased his second home. I like that Jabari wants to better himself. I wonder if the wild life of his was anything like my hoe phase.

    Pulling up to the Morton's, I became nervous all over again. I'm really about to have my first real date in a long time. I didn't realize that Jabari had gotten out of the car and opened my door already. I took a deep breath and stepped out of the car. Once inside, Jabari told the waitress our reservations and she had us follow her to our table. My palms started to get sweaty, so I kept them under the table. Jabari leans in and says, "Just breathe, I'm not gonna bite". I let out a laugh and everything was better from there. Once we ordered our drinks and food, the rest was filled with conversations. He asked multiple questions about myself and I answered very bluntly but still kept a mystery. Can't let him in all the way. I spoke about my childhood, adult life, work life, social life, my goals and passions. He tried to be slick and throw in flings only because he was comfortable enough to explain that was one of the reasons for leaving Vegas. I let him know I had my fun but kept it at that.

    At the end of dinner, he asked if I wanted to continue the date because he was having a good time and didn't want it to end. I was happy that I kept his attention and he enjoyed my company. I told him yes the date can continue. Jabari paid the bill and as we're walking to the car, he wanted to know if I wanted dessert. I laughed at the thought in my head. If only he knew the old me would say, only if you have something I can lick on. I went along with that thought though and said yes to dessert and that I was thinking Ben&Jerry's. If eyes could talk, they would be saying he's excited to see how I lick ice cream. The expression didn't last long because he tried to hide it, but he agreed to ice cream. With everything being downtown, we went to get our dessert then he drove to the waterfront, and we walked along the water. Jabari noticed how relaxed I became. "You're breathing normal. Water must be your peace?" I stopped in my tracks because no one has ever paid that much attention to me to notice something so small. I told Jabari that water is my happy place, whenever there is something going on in my life, the waterfront is the first place I come to, then it's Multnomah Falls, and if I feel like driving far then I'll go to Seaside. I let him know that nature grounds me.

    We decided to wrap up the night when we noticed the time. It was after midnight. Between dinner and our walk with amazing conversation, time passed us by. I honestly didn't want the date to end but I feel like I will be seeing more of Jabari. As we approached the car, Jabari said he hopes there will be more nights like this. Is this man in my head? Thinking the thought and him saying it, gave me more butterflies. I smiled and told him I can make that happen. In the car ride home, the unexpected happened. As I'm looking out the window at the clear night sky, I felt Jabari's hand reaching to hold my hand. I turned to look at him and took his hand in. With the slow jams playing in the background, this felt like a scene from a romance movie where we gazed into each other's eyes and not focus on the road. But neither one of us is that corny.

Pulling up to the house, I looked at the time and noticed it was one in the morning. Part of me didn't want the night to end. I wanted to invite him in. Not for anything sexual but for more of his time. Jabari brought that part of my life I kept away for months back to life. I think I'm going to take a chance. As Jabari opens my door and opens his arms for a hug, I look towards the house and ask if he wants to come in. The look on his face was surprising but he surprised me by saying yes. I looked up while we walked to the door and saw Michelle peaking out her window. That girl is always nosy, damn I wanted to give her the tea about Jabari continuing the night in my room, but now she knows. Once in the house, I asked him to wait by the stairs while I grabbed some drinks and snacks from the kitchen. Now it's time to go upstairs and see how much control I have over myself.

"So no TV, just a soundbar. You must really love music that much, or watching shows just isn't your thing", Jabari said as he stepped into my room. I grabbed a remote to turn on my projector and he was amazed. I laughed and told him there wasn't a

TV big enough to fill my wall. I like to feel like I'm at the movies. Jabari noticed the bean bag chair and sat on it. If this is his way of being respectful, that's perfectly fine with me. I laid at the edge of my bed right next to his shoulder and leaned on it. I don't know what made me do it but it felt right. He leaned his head on my head and suggested we watch a movie or play music. I went to youtube and put on my slow jams playlist and we just talked. Jabari became more comfortable and decided to lay on the bed with me. I didn't get uncomfortable. I surprised myself by laying on his chest while talking. Feeling his fingers twirling in my curls, made me want to take his dick into my mouth. His touch is sensible, I can feel the goosebumps forming on my body. While Jabari was talking to me, I noticed his words slurring a bit. I looked up at him and saw his eyes dropping. I grabbed my blanket and covered us and fell asleep in his arms.

When I woke up, Jabari's eyes were looking right at me. He smiled and said, "I didn't want to wake you, even though you were laying on my arm and cut off my circulation a little bit.". I laughed and sat up so he could grab his arm. Jabari asked if I had a good time and I told him yes. If he knew that I dreamed about him eating the fuck out of my pussy and ass and wished that it really happened, my night would have ended perfect. I walked Jabari to the front door once he got himself together. He leaned over and kissed me on my forehead and let me know he'll text me when he gets settled at home. I watched Jabari walk to his car before closing the door. I wanted to jump up and down but as soon as I turned around, Michelle was standing there smiling ear to ear. I screamed which made her scream along with me. "BITCH WHAT THE FUCK ARE YOU DOING CREEPING UP BEHIND ME LIKE THAT?!" Michelle couldn't do anything but laugh. Of course she wanted the details. "We went to dinner, walked along the waterfront, came here, and went to sleep."

The blank stare on Michelle's face said she's annoyed with my bullshit. Now I'm the one laughing up the stairs to my room to go back to sleep.

Laying in bed, replaying the night over in my head, made me proud of myself. I didn't fuck him, suck him, sit on his face. I just laid in his arms. Even though I did dream about him and woke up to my pussy soaking, I'm still proud of myself. When I checked my phone, Jabari sent me a text. He wrote, "You look so beautiful when you're asleep.". I opened the message to respond and there was a picture of me sleeping with my mouth wide open.

He ain't shit! But I'm not mad at him, I'll get him back, if I get the chance to see him again. Which I'm sure I will.

Over the next few days, Jabari and I talked nonstop. The conversation of meeting up again never came back up and I didn't like that. I wanted to see him again but didn't want to come off thirsty. The girls kept telling me to forget about it, if he wants to see me, he'll ask. I'll let him be, for now. Usually Jabari and I will text or talk on the phone from the start of the day to the end of the night. But today I decided to do something different. I woke up to a good morning text from Jabari and decided not to respond. I can't make myself available to him. I don't care how good of a first date we had. I can't give him all my time.

I went to work, then afterwards out to a bar for a needed drink and some food. When I got back home, Nala and Zuri were over cooking with Michelle in the kitchen. Zuri came running to me and I welcomed her in my arms. Nala walked over and instantly went into talking about dating some guy from her job. Why do my friends think I'm lonely only because one guy hasn't asked to see me again?! Nala went on and on about this man's credentials and I blocked her out by playing with Zuri.

My phone vibrated and it was a text from Lawrence.

Lawrence
Tomorrow is Jabari's birthday and he doesn't want to do anything. Maybe you can get him out of the house?

Now why do I have to be the one to celebrate him? I just realized how close our birthdays are. That's besides the point. Jabari has been texting me all this time and not once has he mentioned his birthday. I couldn't decide if I was going to ask him about it but I did want to see him. I decided to text him and ask what he had planned for the night and that I want to see if he was free to hang. I went back to playing with Zuri while telling Nala to let it go. I understand my friend's concern but just because I got my feet wet once doesn't mean this is going to happen often. My phone vibrated and reading the text, my jaw dropped.

Jabari
My birthday is tomorrow but how about you coming over to pre celebrate. You come over, eat some food, then I eat your pussy.

The way I almost dropped my goddaughter off my lap, had Nala ready to cuss me out. I apologized while showing Nala and Michelle the text. Michelle for the shit and said to bust the pussy open while Nala being the mother figure and judging. I told them both to have a good night because I'm about to get ready for my night. I text Jabari back telling him to send his address just to see if he's serious. When I saw this man text me back fast as hell, I wasn't even expecting it that quick.

As I'm looking for something to wear, I feel my anxiety starting to creep up. My thoughts were racing. What if this is something I don't need? What if I decide to start a rotation back up if he isn't satisfying me? What if he doesn't even eat my pussy and just messing with me? Maybe he is testing me and seeing if I'm only going over thinking I want to fuck. I thought to myself, "Nomi, you're thirty fucking years old! If you want to fuck, then go fuck!". I'm going to go fuck Jabari.

After showering and getting dressed, I let him know I will be on the way. Nala was side-eyeing me as I was walking down the stairs. "Nala look, I haven't been pleased in a long time. I wanted to let loose and you or anyone else can stop me or make me feel some type of way. I'm grown and I will be fine.". Nala hugged me while Michelle in the background yelling to go get that dick. These two are definitely the angel and demon friends. I love it though. I picked up Zuri and hugged her before stepping out. Once in the car, I put on my "In The Mood" playlist to bring out all the hornyness I've been feeling since Jabari came into my life. My pussy was heating up on this drive to his place. It's almost like my pussy is talking to me, happy that we might get some action tonight. Honestly, I need this. Nine months of nothing, it's time to break this celibacy.

When I pulled up to Jabari's place, I sat in the car for ten minutes to get myself together. He ended up texting me asking if I was close. I responded that I'm in the parking lot, and I'm starting to walk up. As I'm approaching his door, he was already standing outside. Damn, why did he have to step outside in some gray sweats and no shirt on? Jabari pulled me in for a hug and held me tight before taking his hand on my ass and guiding me inside his place.

The instant smell of steak and mashed potatoes cooking made my mouth water. Jabari asked how I like my steak, and I told him medium well. While we were talking he said make myself comfortable. "If you want to sit on the counter, go right ahead and do that. Whatever you want to do, do it." I decided to sit on the counter just to see if he's testing me. Jabari didn't mind at all.

We had a great conversation while he was cooking. Jabari was so focused on me, I didn't even know that anything was in the oven until I looked at it and saw that it was on. I asked what was in the oven and he yelled "SHIT!" so loud. During our conversation, I mentioned that I can't stand chewy asparagus and that's exactly what he forgot he was cooking. I couldn't do anything but laugh. Jabari came between my legs and put his hands on my side tickling me and I begged him to stop. He said fine and kissed my cheek. This man is too smooth for me. When he fixed our plates, and sat them on the table, I noticed he set out a bottle of wine. I decided to set the glasses out and pour some wine into the glasses. Jabari turned around and saw me holding both the glasses and he smiled. I sat them on the table and he pulled my chair out so I could sit down. I didn't notice that he lit the two candles and dimmed the lights.

    Jabari thanked me for coming over and having a pre birthday celebration with him. He explained he usually goes out with family or friends but this year being in a new state, he just kept his birthday to himself. Jabari didn't want me to even know because he was itching for some affection and didn't know how to be smooth about inviting me over. I repeated his text to him and he laughed because how smooth can you be about inviting a woman over saying you're going to cook for her and eat her pussy. He told me to just let the night go with the flow. Whatever happens, happens.

I complimented his cooking skills and said everything was good. With my mind focusing on trying to get some dick, I didn't eat too much. I noticed he did the same. He grabbed both plates, then led me to the couch. I noticed every move he made was thought through. The movie he planned for us to watch was already on the screen, Poetic Justice.

Sitting on the couch started off awkward as fuck. We both sat on each end as if this was the first time ever meeting. I chugged my glass of wine and went to pour another to ease my nerves. I felt myself becoming more comfortable as I sipped this second wine glass. Unexpectedly I leaned over and laid on Jabari's chest and I heard his heart beating faster. What is he nervous for? He is the one that said he wanted to eat my pussy. With me laying on Jabari, I can tell he was relaxing his nerves. He leaned over and kissed me on my forehead and thanked me for coming over. I sat up and looked at him and smiled.

Next thing I know his lips were on mine and we were in a full make out session. The way he was working his tongue in my mouth, woke up my pussy and I felt her getting wetter by the minute. Jabari removed himself from my lips and started slowly kissing on my neck. His hand was squeezing my breast before he started playing the violin with my nipple. Everything felt amazing, and his touch had me moaning for more. I noticed his hand leaving my breast and heading down south. As his hand reached into my pants, I grabbed his hand. I don't know what came over me but I felt like this was moving too fast. Jabari looked at me and said that we can stop. The thing is, I didn't want him to stop, I want to feel everything he has to offer.

I took Jabari's hand and led it to my clit. The rest was history. I haven't been touched in a very long time, one finger to my clit and I'm moaning loud as fuck. I was so sensitive, it feels like I already had an orgasm. Jabari lifted my shirt and took my titties out my bra and started sucking on my nipple, while still playing with my pussy. The moaning of his name made him go insane. I didn't realize that he left my nipple alone until I felt his tongue licking my pussy juices. The real question is when did he get my pants off?

I became so lost in my thoughts, and had to turn my brain off until he surprised me by flipping me onto my back and started tongue fucking my ass. If Jabari knew it's been almost a year since I've had any action, I don't think he would do all of this. He's about to have me hooked on him and I haven't even got the dick yet. With two fingers in my pussy and a tongue in my ass, the moans stayed loud. I hope his neighbors don't mind because they will definitely know his name after tonight.

Jabari made me have the best orgasm from only foreplay that I didn't want the dick anymore. I wanted to sleep the night away. He helped me up and led me to the bedroom. There were candles lit and a red light on. Looks like he is looking for that red light special. He turned on some music and the first song to come on was Pleasure P Lick Lick Lick. I laughed in my head because that used to be my go to song before getting laid. Jabari asked me to lay on top of him.

While my head was right under his beard, the smell of my pussy was soaking it up beautifully. I started rubbing it and he laughed lightly as if he was shocked that I was enjoying the smell. I mean it's me on his beard and I know I smell and taste good. The feeling of his dick jumping underneath me, made me give him a look like can you be serious right now. Jabari lifted me up a little bit to get from under me, to get behind me. I arched my back and he took one hand to pin me down to the bed by my neck and entered my pussy. Each stroke had me crying out for more.

The way Jabari was fucking me was going to have me dickmatized and I don't think I'm going to like that. The spreading of my ass to make his dick go deeper in me, feeling every inch, had me throwing my ass back. I'm going to guess that was too much for him to handle because he put us in a missionary position, holding my legs up, rearranging my insides any way he could. It feels like he's hitting areas I didn't know were able to be hit. Plus I noticed that his dick is slightly curved and it's curving perfectly with my pussy. The more he was stroking, he started growling and it turned me on, to the point I felt my juices soaking more on the bed. Jabari yelled he's about to cum. He leaned over and started sucking on my nipple and I moaned his name and that did it. Jabari pulled out and busted all on my chest. He got up and went into the bathroom and came out with a wet towel. Jabari wiped me off and wiped my pussy and ass down. Well this is something new and different for me.

Afterwards we laid in bed and talked. I noticed Jabari was dosing off, so I decided to get dressed. Once dressed, I walked back to the bed to wake Jabari up to come lock his door. He got out of bed and his dick is just standing up looking at me. He noticed me staring and smiled as he was grabbing a pair of shorts to put on to walk me to my car.

When we reached my car, he pulled me in for a hug then kissed me goodbye. Jabari told me to let him know when I get home. As I started to head out of his apartments, I looked in the rearview, I saw him still standing outside until I got too far out and noticed him walking back towards his place. Now I can breathe. I can't believe how this night went. From delicious food to amazing dick. I gave in after almost putting a stop to it. I like that I kept it going. My body needed this, everything was what I needed to experience.

I realized I was punishing my body instead of setting boundaries. I took my rehab and looked at things the wrong way. I only had to ease up on how I was using my body, giving it to multiple men. My thoughts are all over the place. Maybe I will set up a session with Dr. Johnson and we can discuss this. Actually I will do that. This is my first time letting loose since walking into rehab. Time for the reassurance to not question myself too much.

Pulling up to the house, I noticed all my girls' cars parked outside. Not Michelle having everyone over to discuss how my night went. Or maybe it was Nala being concerned and wanted to do a slight intervention. It's 2am and I'm tired and want to sleep. I text Jabari letting him know I made it home. Walking inside was already dreadful to the point it has me considering getting my own spot because this is too much.

I've spent months locked up in my room. I only go to work and come back home. My social anxiety became too much to bear. Now that I've stepped out for my birthday and went on a date and got some dick now everyone wants to be concerned. I spent three months in rehab, I've learned a lot. Clearly I did, if I spent the last six months in hiding. Let me handle this craziness before I get mad.

"Before you say anything to any of us, this was Nala's doing. Michelle tried to talk her out of it but she didn't want to listen.", said Tiana.

"I was on my way to sleep and Nala made it sound so urgent until I pulled up and realized it was bullshit!", said Chloe.

"And I was busy bouncing on some dick my damn self but like Chloe said Nala made it seem urgent.", said Renee.

"I didn't want to come, I was forced. Nala made Chloe pick me up.", said Ashley.

"You know damn well I was encouraging you to go wild, even when you didn't want to. I was on your side tonight while Nala wanted to play mama bear.", said Michelle

"So all of y'all going to turn on me right now? Yes I was concerned but it was for a good cause. I can tell by the look on your face, you're annoyed with me, but hear me out. I married young, I had Zuri right after getting married. You know damn well I had my share of men and went wild but I stopped when I found Elijah. I'm not saying you're going to have another hoe phase, but you going to rehab was serious and I want you to see how serious it was. You meet Jabari and you guys hit it off right away. Who is to say, you meet someone else and things go smooth and next thing you know you have a roster going again. It's your life and I'm not judging you but I want you to think things through. The excitement you had ready to leave to go get some dick was concerning and I care about you. That's it, that's all." said Nala.

I really couldn't believe all I was hearing. I just knew I was going to come home and go to sleep extra satisfied but I have to deal with this shit. I knew this was Nala's doing but damn this bitch really coming at me like this. And the fact she expected anyone to have her back? We all snitch on each other when it comes to things we know are pointless. You know what, I had a great night and I'm not going to let them ruin it. I got some of the best dick that I had in awhile. I had a couple orgasms. Amazing tongue on my pussy. I'm on cloud nine right now.

I kept my response short and sweet and said, "If you guys choose to stay the night, by all means you know where the blankets are. I had a great night and I'm going to sleep peacefully. Nala please go home to your husband and stop stressing about me. I'm good, seriously. I don't have time for this and don't need my night ruined. Goodnight and I love y'all.".

I walked up the stairs and shut my door and locked it. I'm letting it be known I don't want anyone to bother me. I couldn't react the way I wanted to because we would all be up until the crack of dawn and none of us needed that. I went to charge my phone and noticed that Nala texted me.

Nala

Nomi I'm sorry. I didn't mean to ambush you like that. I was just being a concerned, worried friend and took it too far. I love you girl. Elijah is on his way to get me. I'll hit you up later this week to do lunch.

I know Nala meant no harm but sometimes I wish she would just focus on only being Zuri's mom and not the rest of ours. I didn't have the energy to respond so I only hearted the text. I checked to see if Jabari responded and he did by telling me he had a great night and that he's going to sleep like a baby. I left him on read and went to sleep. My dreams came instantly but I couldn't remember anything except for seeing a head between my legs. I woke up and felt between my legs and I was wetter than the damn ocean, if that's even possible. When I checked the time, it was six in the morning. Nomi take your ass back to sleep, I thought to myself.

When I officially woke up it was twelve noon. I wasn't sure who I was going to see coming down the stairs but as long as Nala was gone from the house, I wouldn't trip too much on the rest of the girls. Nala and I need to have a private conversation. The first person I saw coming down the stairs was Michelle. She let me know everyone had gone home a couple hours ago. I'm glad it's just me and her. And I already know she is going to want the tea but she also knows when I get ambushed, I shut down until I'm ready to come back around.

"So you are not going to tell me about last night because girl, I know Jabari put it on you for you to respond so calmly to Nala's bullshit. We were all pissed. And Renee was ready to cuss her out because you know how that girl gets over her man and having to leave him to deal with some petty shit."

I rolled my eyes, and told her ass fuck no, I'm not saying shit. I was mad at Michelle a little bit because I expected her to at least send me a warning text. I did tell Michelle that I'm thinking about getting my own place. I could tell that it broke her heart but last night did something to me. It could be the anger talking because I really do enjoy living with Michelle. Once I cool down, we can have a conversation. I went back upstairs to my room to shower and get ready for the day. I started my shower and the thought of Jabari touching me, relaxed me. That man has a way with his hands. I closed my eyes and replayed the night in my head. The slight moan I let out brought me back to reality. I got in the shower and focused on one goal I had for the day. I'm going to call Dr. Johnson and set up an appointment. I'm sure he would be shocked to hear from me.

After getting out of the shower, I went to my phone and called Dr. Johnson. He answered so fast, his schedule must be open today. I let him know that I would like to make an appointment and he told me he has time in the next hour if I'm available to see him. I told him yes and that I'll see him soon. I hung up and dried off and started to get dressed. Coming back down the stairs, Michelle was sitting on the couch. "I love you girl, I'm about to go see Dr. Johnson and when I get back, we can make drinks and talk about last night.". The smile on her face was all I wanted to see.

Michelle has been through enough during our friendship. The house we stay in is actually her parent's house. She lost her dad to gun violence, while he was trying to stop the altercation between two men. Her mother passed away a month after that incident. She died of a broken heart. Her parents were childhood loves that met at the age of ten years old. All they knew were each other. When they passed, Michelle was left with a trust fund and her parents house. I was with her through everything. Our friendship also started at the age of ten. And we have been stuck like glue since then.

    As I'm walking to the car, I receive a phone call from Jabari. I let it go to voicemail, and text him to let him know that I'm busy and I will call him back once I'm free. I needed a clear mind on the way to see Dr. Johnson and Jabari is the last person I need to talk to before this appointment. I'm glad I was able to keep Dr. Johnson as a therapist. I opened up to him about my many sexual experiences and he helped me take control, I think. And that is exactly why I'm heading to see him now. Pulling up to the facility is giving me chills. The only difference is I'm not checking myself in. I don't have to stay here for three months. As I'm walking towards the doors, I notice Dr. Johnson came to greet me.

    "Nomi! It's so nice to see you again."

    I smiled and thanked him again for seeing me on short notice. We walked to his office and once the doors were closed behind me, all my stories that I told him came all rushing at once. From my back hall days in high school, to losing my virginity to a friend, to my Chicago trip of fucking a hotel employee on the first night of being there. Yes, there's many more but it's like I burned a hole in his couch telling everything.

"So tell me Nomi, How is everything going? Haven't heard from you in about seven months. I hope you got back readjusted to the world outside of these walls."

I let him know that in the last month, I actually started to live a little. I told him how I turned thirty and met a guy. I went on a date with him, then last night I went over to his place and got intimate with him. The look on Dr. Johnson's face never fails me. I explained how I did stop at first to think about it. But the opportunity presented itself and I jumped on it. No man has touched me since I left this facility, I don't even care to pleasure myself because I was too much in my head.

I left here thinking that I'm supposed to give up sex and be a nun. I was scared to do anything, let alone talk to a man. Do you know that I was hiding from men? I was treating myself out at the earliest hour to avoid any type of contact. My social anxiety became overwhelming and I stayed out of the way. I was terrified of reversing all that I learned. Then it hit me, you were teaching to value myself, that I don't have to give it up to every man that says hi. That I don't have to have a special man for each thing that they offer the best of. I can take control and I did that. Like I said, last night I stopped him but I wanted it, so I gave him the green light.

Dr. Johnson applauded me on coming to terms on what he was trying to teach me that I misunderstood. He also reminded me that it's me against me. How I want to feel about my decision is only for me to know. But he told me that once I make that decision, I can't dwell and start to think of other scenarios of how it could have gone. He went on to tell me to come out of hiding for good. I spent six months bottling myself under a rock, being in hermit mode. He hopes this one experience gives me some clarity and a better understanding of how to go about things.

I thanked Dr. Johnson for still being here to help and guide me when needed. Part of me felt like I was losing my mind but he told me it's expected to be lost in the beginning when you leave the facility because of your fears of relapsing. I can understand that. That's exactly what I did, let my fears take over instead of living differently. My session has come to an end and I hugged Dr. Johnson. I thanked him for everything. This time walking out of the building, I felt more confident in my future decisions. The past needs to be left behind, and I need to bring both feet to the present.

I got in the car and took off. I was in a better mood than earlier, and it's showing. I decided to stop by the store to pick up some items for tonight. I was a little hard on Michelle so I needed to make it up to her. I grabbed all of our favorite snacks, then moved onto the liquor aisle. I feel like this should be a wine type of night, anything harder and it'll be tears flowing and that's not what neither one of us need to be on. I grabbed three bottles of champagne and pineapple and cranberry juice.

As I'm scanning aisles to see if there is anything else I need, I hear someone call my name. I turn around and to my surprise it's Jabari. The feeling of my pussy throbbing took over instantly. Fuck having butterflies in my stomach, they're all in my pussy ready to be released like an orgasm.

"Hello beautiful, looks like you're going to have a fun night.", Jabari said while looking in my basket. I looked down and agreed. My cart has pizzas, chips, cookies, and champagne in it. I told Jabari that Michelle and I are gonna have a roommate night. Been awhile since we relaxed and just laughed the night away. We're both always busy or always having company over. I let Jabari know that I was going to call him once I was done shopping. He reassured me that it's okay, he only had a question for me. "Do you like doing yoga?". I shook my head yes. Jabari pulled me in closer and asked, "Do you like doing yoga, naked?".

My eyes became wide and I laughed nervously and told him I've never thought about it. "Maybe you can come over tomorrow night and we do some yoga?". This man asking me to do naked yoga? Shit, you only live once. I told Jabari yes, and that I'll call him to let him know what time I'm free. We walked to the registers together and he helped me clear out my cart. When it came time to pay, he passed me a card. He told me not to say no, and it should cover everything. I noticed he only had two items. I passed them to the cashier and then tapped the card. I thanked him while he was helping put the bags in the car. He responded by saying he'll see me tomorrow night at eight o'clock.

Pulling back up to the house, I noticed that Nala's car was here. This girl just doesn't stop. I let her know that we can plan something later on this week and she had to come over. This better not be Michelle's doing either. I checked my phone to see if I missed a text and I did. Michelle sent me a text saying Nala just popped up. I noticed it was sent ten minutes ago. My mood is still good and I won't let her ruin it. I got out of the car and walked up to the house slowly like I'm already expecting an earful. Opening the house door, I was expecting Zuri to come running to me like she always does.

"Zuri is not here, Nomi. And we're in the kitchen.

Great now I have to actually pay attention, I thought to myself with a slight laugh. I walked into the kitchen with the bags and Nala said she didn't know we were having a girls night and that she'll call the other girls over. Before I could even speak, Michelle said, "It's not a girls night, it's only Nomi and I. No one else. Everyone was here last night and frankly I'm tired and not in the mood for company tonight. You popping up unannounced has got to stop too."

I looked over at Michelle and noticed she was beyond fed up but never cared to say anything. I wanted to hug my girl but I'll wait to do that. Nala was in complete shock. I can tell something was going on with her. But I wanted this night to be about me and Michelle so I had to get Nala going.

"Hey girl let me walk you to your car while we talk about our lunch date."

Michelle started putting the groceries together as me and Nala were walking outside. I hugged Nala letting her know Michelle meant no harm, but she still has to respect our household. Nala nodded. She started to cry and said she caught Elijah cheating and that she uses us as her escape but noticed she was being overly aggressive with me and my situation with Jabari and it wasn't meant to be that way. My jaw dropped. I can't believe that Elijah cheated. Nala and Elijah seemed so perfect. But I can't lie and say after Zuri was born, Nala changed up completely. It's like she put being a mother over everything.

    The girl forgot that she's a wife, and she did stop catering to her husband. Then she started spending more time at our house. Elijah had to take care of himself like he was a bachelor. So I'm not happy he cheated but I'm also not surprised. Nala explained they are about to start therapy. She forgives him and wants to fix it and he wants to do the same. I told her to go home to Elijah and start putting in work now.

    As Nala was driving off, I went back inside and Michelle asked me if I was surprised. I guess that's why Nala came over and we just sent her away. I noticed that the bottles of champagne were on the living room table along with all the snacks. Michelle was ready to start this night more than me. As soon as we got comfortable on the couch, I started off the conversation. I let Michelle know that I don't want to move out, I was only upset about being ambushed last night even though it wasn't an actual intervention, it was still annoying. "Nomi, I knew your mind was going to change about moving out. You don't pay rent! Where are you going?" Michelle said while laughing at me. She does have a point because it's hard out here! Now for the juicy tea Michelle's been waiting for. I filled her in about my night with Jabari and her mouth was stuck open.

"So he wants to do naked yoga tomorrow night?! Is fuckin' involved?"

I rolled my eyes because she knows damn well fuckin' is involved. I told her how something about him makes my pussy ready for all he has to offer. Michelle mentioned how she was supposed to have a fling last night but with Nala doing all that she did, she had to reschedule. I questioned her on who is she even talking to enough to get dicked down because Michelle picky as fuck. "So you know your boy, Lawrence? We hit it off on your birthday. At first, I thought he was slightly annoying but he's not that bad once I got to know him."

Why do my friends choose to give me heart attacks? I didn't have anything to say. Lawrence is not a bad guy, it's just unexpected. I told her to leave me out of it, and to not suggest any double date ideas because Lawrence and Jabari are cousins. One thing Michelle and I always agree on if we're talking to guys that are friends or family to never do double dates. That's not our thing. We spent the rest of the night drowning in mimosas, which turned into lots of laughs and some tears. I'm forever grateful for our friendship.

I'm not from Portland but we moved here when I was ten from Chicago, and the first day of fifth grade Michelle was the first one that approached me. From middle school through high school on to college we've been inseparable. My parents moved back to Chicago after I started college. The plan was to go once I graduated high school but I got accepted into Portland State University and ended up staying. I visit them every chance I get. The rest of the girls came along in high school except for Renee, I met her in college.

I looked over at Michelle and saw her slumped over. I finished another glass of mimosa and laid it down. My mind instantly started racing about seeing Jabari tomorrow. The thought of naked yoga has me wondering how he even came up with something like this. But I'm interested, I couldn't even say no. The way he fucked me the first time, I can only imagine how this night with him will go. I keep playing that night over in my head.

The thought of it made me step upstairs to my room to pleasure myself. Laying in bed, I spread my lips open to stimulate my clit. Closing my eyes, all I see is Jabari on top of me. Imaging his hands rubbing my body, his lips kissing me from my forehead down to my feet. The more I focused on these thoughts, the more I felt my orgasm about to happen. Thinking about Jabari licking my clit was the icing on the cake. I let out a loud moan as I felt myself release. I couldn't wait to see him again.

From the moment I woke up, I had a bad feeling about today. I woke up feeling a weight on my chest. My first thought to myself was I hope I don't get sick. The next thought was maybe I was nervous to see Jabari again. Michelle also had a slight attitude and she couldn't figure out why. What the fuck is going on today? Even work zoom calls stressed me out. Usually I look forward to the days we have meetings because I can keep my camera off and do anything as I pretend to listen.

But today, the manager wanted all cameras on and wanted us to participate in the conversations. You know how annoying it is to actually have to find clothes to wear when working from home?! I'm always naked. After work was over, I called Jabari to confirm the time and he said I can come anytime after seven. He also asked if I wanted to spend the night because it might be a long night. I didn't decline the offer. But I also said yes too fast. What is this man trying to do?

After getting ready and getting my bag together, I let Michelle know I'll be back in the morning. She was excited because Lawrence will be coming over. I guess this will be a great night for the both of us. I let Jabari know I was on my way. The whole ride to his place was smooth and was looking like this weird energy of a day is turning around. As I'm approaching Jabari's apartments, I get in the turn lane and the unexpected happens. I got rear ended. It wasn't a hard hit, but as soon as I turned my hazards on and got out of the car to check my car, the other car already sped off.

I'm no longer in the mood for anything and want to go back home. Before I could tell Jabari I'm not in the mood, he was already outside looking my way. I turned into his place and parked and explained what happened. He looked at my bumper and said, "not even a scratch, but at least you're okay.".

My mood went from fuck this to what the fuck as I'm walking into his place. There were candles from the front door leading to the living room. He had rain music playing and I became relaxed instantly. Jabari paused the music, and had me sit on the couch. He could tell that I was overwhelmed. He stepped away and came back with his hands full. One hand backwoods and weed. The other had a wine glass. I looked at him and smiled saying that I'll take both. He rolled up and I was sipping until he was done. Let the session begin.

Jabari let me take the first hit, and I inhaled like it's the last time I'll ever smoke. I wanted to leave. I was relaxed by now but my mind is still running. Jabari let me smoke the entire wood by myself. Each time I passed it to him he would take one hit or say that I need it more than him.

After finishing my glass of wine and the wood, I felt like I was floating. My mind was calm. Jabari took my hand and walked me over to where we are doing yoga. He asked if he could undress me. I shook my head yes. He started off with my leggings, then moved along to my shirt, leaving me in my bra and panties. Jabari looked at me and told me that I'm beautiful. He came up to me and kissed my forehead. I felt like I just melted in his arms as he reached behind me to unhook my bra.

Sliding my arms through the straps to release my breast. I slightly started to become a little uncomfortable. This felt more intimate than I imagined. As I stood there stuck in my thoughts, Jabari asked me to get in a lotus position so he could rub my body with hot oil. The feeling of his hands rubbing oil on my nipples made me moan quietly. I'm still trying to find the words to describe how he makes me feel.

During the process of rubbing my body down, he stood me up and put me in a forward fold position. My legs were spread and my upper body was bent over with my hands planted on the blanket. Jabari took his hands down my back before inserting two fingers in my pussy while telling me to stay calm. What the fuck does he mean to stay calm?! Jabari is holding my waist as I'm crying out in pleasure. The moment he takes his fingers out of me, instantly his dick enters and I'm trying to not fall over. The only thought going through my head right now is the way he is fucking me feels like I'm hanging off the side of the bed. My moans became so uncontrollable that I started to slip to the floor.

Right when his dick slides out, my body collapses and we both laugh. When I turned around to look at him, he told me I'm beautiful. Why does this man keep complimenting me during sex? My pussy can't take it. Shit I can't take it. Jabari looks me in my eyes and I once again want to melt away. He leaned in for a kiss but I turned my head away and his lips planted on my neck. I quickly regretted that motion because now the way he is sucking on my neck has me going crazy.

Jabari flipped me back on my stomach and lifted me by my waist and let his dick rub on my clit before going inside of me. My back arched to take that dick how I should. He decided to place a hand on my lower back and that gave a different feeling and me calling out his name showed the difference. It felt like Jabari was growing inside of me and his dick became too much for me to handle. I started to feel my pussy becoming raw and tried to run. He pulled me back towards him and even said to stop running. I yelled that I'm about to cum and he went harder. My breathing became too much to handle as I started to cream on his dick. While I'm in the middle of my orgasm, he pulls out and busts on my ass. Feeling the warmth of semen on my ass always makes me cringe for some reason. But he quickly got up to grab a towel and wiped it off.

    We laid on the blanket for a little bit before helping each other up and going to the bedroom to get more comfortable. As we're laying on the bed, Jabari gets up and heads to his closet. When he comes out, he has a feather in his hand. I asked him what he was going to do with the feather and he said to close my eyes. The moment my eyes were shut, I started to feel the feather on my body, starting at my feet. It was a tickling but a sensational feeling. The feather circling around my nipples, especially the right one, made me clinch the sheets. When he approached my pussy, he let the tip of the feather tickle my clit. The more I moaned loudly, I felt myself about to climax. I became so sensitive towards the feather, I didn't notice he had stopped with the feather and his tongue was flicking my clit.

I felt everything in me about to explode and I couldn't help myself. Jabari spread my thighs farther apart and stuffed his face in my pussy going insane with his tongue. I yelled I was about to cum and his tongue started moving faster. The more sensitive I became the more I tried to move away but he held me down. I let out the loudest scream and creamed all over his beard. When Jabari looked at me, his beard was dripping of my juices. I did the unexpected and smelled his beard and told him it smells good. He couldn't do anything but laugh. We got comfortable in bed and he held me until we fell asleep.

When I woke up to check the time, it was three in the morning. I tried to slide out the bed quietly to get dressed but failed. I turned around to see Jabari sitting up. "You know, you don't have to leave. You can stay." I was shocked and didn't know what to say. I'm the type to come get what I want and leave. I've never fallen asleep anywhere but in my own bed. Part of me wanted to leave but my body laid back down besides him. He wrapped me in tight and we went back to sleep.

Driving home had me in my thoughts. I really left this man's house at ten this morning. Never in my life have I ever done this. Jabari cooked me breakfast too. I woke up to French toast, eggs over medium, and sausage patties with a mimosa on the side. I can't wait to talk to Michelle and tell her everything that went down. Actually she'll probably be happy that I stayed because she was having Lawrence over. This is only the third meet up and we're having yoga sex now? I don't know where to start with my thoughts.

When I got home, Lawrence was walking to his car. I got out of the car and he instantly tried to explain himself. I laughed and let him know I'm no better since I have been hanging out with Jabari. "Please be careful with him. He's smooth with the ladies and his charm can make a woman feel like she's falling for him. You're my friend, yes he's family but you matter to me too." I thanked him and sent him on his way. I'll think about that later.

As I'm walking into the house, Michelle is laid out on the couch in her own world. She sat up as soon as she heard the door close and that was the end of her deep thoughts. We both looked at each other and knew tea was about to be spilled. Since Michelle already knew about yoga night, I filled her in on how it was. The look on her face was very confusing because I'm giving juicy details and she looks like she wants to cry. "Nomi I'm jealous! Jabari has amazing dick and great tongue and knows how to satisfy you! Lawrence on the other hand is disappointing. Great size dick but he doesn't know how to work it! The tongue game is amazing but you know I love to feel the dick inside of me. All I can say is that dick is going to waste and it doesn't make any sense. I seriously want to cry!"

    I couldn't do anything but hug my girl and laugh too. Michelle had to learn the hard way. During my hoe phase, she never understood completely why I had different men instead of dealing with one. Each one that I dealt with offered something the other couldn't. I was satisfied in many ways. Michelle is the type to get hooked onto one person and try her hardest to fix everything about them sexually. She enjoys being the teacher even if the man doesn't learn. So I know Lawrence is her next student. After catching up about our night and early morning, we went our separate ways. I needed to shower and clear my mind. Jabari has me feeling all kinds of ways.

Over the next few weeks, Jabari and I became almost inseparable. I saw him at least four times a week. Each time he invited me over, I ended up staying the night. The sex became more intense. But it was more than sex. Our conversations were deep. We got to know each other on another level. It never failed, when I would go to his place, dinner was being prepared. Then a movie would follow up next while cuddling on the couch. And once that movie was over, we went to bed. Depending on how the day went prior to me coming over, I would shower before getting in bed with him. Mind you it's still summer, so I'm out in the sun with my girls. Then I head to Jabari's place after a day out drinking and eating good.

One day Jabari was making plans for me to come over but plans had changed because he's supposed to have his friends over. While I stepped out with the girls to enjoy some sushi, I received a text from Jabari saying plans have changed and I can still come over as planned. Renee asked what if there's another female he's fucking on and thats why he cancelled with me but then the other one had to cancel so now he's back to wanting your company. I never thought of the fact of Jabari dealing with anyone else because we're not exclusive.

Also only been dealing with each other for a couple months. And I never thought to ask him if he's entertaining anyone else besides me. Why is this girl trying to get me to think? But if I'm thinking about it, does that mean I have feelings developing for him? I can't remember the last time I actually expressed feelings for anyone. All I know is, I'm hooked and don't want it to stop.

"So I think I have a problem. On days when I know I'm going to be chilling with Jabari, I've had old flings hit me up. At first, I tell them I'm down to hang out and right when I get a call or text from Jabari, I cancel with them and go see him. I think I might be catching feelings for him. I'm not sure what it is but this has me feeling weird. Y'all know that my heart is numb to love but he has me feeling all mushy inside."

All eyes were on me, even Zuri looked at me like she understood. Part of me wishes I never said anything. Nala said to follow my mind but protect my heart. Everyone else agreed with her. All I can think about is how I went from this sex addict looking for multiple ways to be satisfied to rehab to catching feelings for the first person I decided to break my celibacy to. It's like I'm a virgin all over again. The only difference is I didn't even have feelings for the person I lost my virginity to! I'm just going to live in the moment. The best option at this moment is to not overthink too much. I let the girls know I will take it slow with Jabari.

Imagine telling your girls you'll take it slow but still continue seeing the guy three days a week. I went from four days down to three. That's taking it slow for me. Jabari and I never stepped out anywhere, unless it was the grocery store. This man kept me fed with home cooked meals. If that's his way of keeping me around, it's working. Michelle keeps wondering why Jabari doesn't take me out on dates anymore. We've only been on two and all the other nights have been spent at his place. It doesn't bother me so I don't know why she's concerned. Besides, eating at home saves money and it tastes better too.

During one of our nights laying in bed after a round of shots of tequila, we decided to play a game of truth and dare. Jabari quickly said he will always do the truth. Without thinking, I asked him is he fucking anyone else. I covered my mouth so fast, shocked that I even asked that question. The look on Jabari's face was stunned but I was even more stunned by his answer. "Yes and no. I was when we first started but now it's just you. Some of the women started acting weird and lying over bullshit. I almost cut you off too but couldn't bring myself to do it. And that is the truth."

    I sat there in silence. When I finally had the words to speak, Jabari beat me to the punch. He suggested that we cut the night short and that I should go home. I didn't respond, I only gathered my things and left. When I got in the car, my mind started racing. What the fuck was I thinking?! We're not exclusive, a couple, talking stage, whatever you want to call it. Just two people fucking and having a good time. I let my feelings get the best of me and it's showing. I texted Jabari to let him know that it was just a general question and I didn't mean to make things awkward. I drove home in silence. Walking through the door, Michelle popped up from the couch and looked at me and all she did was say we'll talk tomorrow. I went to my room and fell asleep.

It's been two weeks since I've heard from Jabari. He fell off the face of the earth. I can't believe that conversation scared him off. I did text a few times but didn't get any response. It was a friday night and I hit the girls up to come through for a girl's night. Something about having drinks seemed right to get my mind off Jabari. Michelle wasn't in the mood, Nala said she needs to focus on her marriage, Renee had a booty call, Ashley, Chloe, and Tiana are sick. Looks like I'm going solo tonight. I'll be going to my favorite sushi spot, with my favorite bartender pouring strong drinks.

Walking into Uchu, I froze at the front door. Why the fuck is Jabari sitting at the bar? The entire time we were hanging out, we never went anywhere! Now he wants to step out. I wanted to turn around and leave but my feet kept moving towards the bar. "Nomi, long time since you've been here!".

Jabari turned around right when he heard my name. He looked like a deer in headlights. I did my best to ignore him even though I wanted to fold. As I'm talking to the bartender, Jabari walks over and asks if we can talk. I wanted to tell him no but I also wanted to know why he has been distant. "Nomi before you say anything, let me explain. After our talk, I had to remove myself from you. I felt that your feelings were getting involved and that's not what I need to happen. We were supposed to be having fun, enjoying each other's company. You asking me about fucking on someone else, made me look at you like I'm giving you too much of my time. But I miss having you around and maybe we can get back to just having fun."

I asked Jabari to please leave me alone. The bullshit he just fed me doesn't make any sense to me. Just because I asked him if he was fucking anyone else?! At least he was honest, he could've lied to me but I didn't know that would make him so uncomfortable. Jabari wanted to talk it out but I asked him to let me be. I let him know if I felt like talking, I'll reach out. As I sat there enjoying my drinks and sushi, I called Michelle asking her to come join me. The sound of my voice had her popping up in the next fifteen minutes.

When Michelle walked in, Jabari was walking out. Michelle came over all giggly until she saw my face. Michelle knew what it looked like when my feelings were crushed. She knew that my heart was numb for years. I never gave anyone the satisfaction to get that close to me. Jabari got close and I fell for him. And the feeling wasn't mutual. It was a great few months. Michelle asked for two shots of tequila and we cheered to moving on. When it came to paying the bill, my bartender said that it was covered. I'm shocked that Jabari covered my bill but not too surprised. Maybe I'll reach out to him again but now, going back to focusing on me.

Two months have passed since I've spoken to Jabari. He reached out once and I left him on read. Maybe I overreacted but I took Lawrence's advice and protected myself. It was for the best. I'm thankful for that experience though. I can't complain about great sex that's for sure, but the main thing was I learned I can't always be available. I don't need my feelings getting involved and crushed in the process.

    Everyone around me is thriving and I'm happy for them. Michelle and Lawrence became a couple. Nala's marriage is doing better. Couples therapy is doing great for them. My side hustle is picking up too with the holiday season approaching. Photography will always be my first and only love. Now if I can make some real money off of it, I'll quit my day job. With everything going smoothly with me and focusing on self love and taking care of myself, I wanted to treat myself to a vacation. I decided to surprise my parents in Chicago. I went ahead and booked my flight then called my mom. I let her know what days I'll be there.

"Nomi don't be upset but your dad and I are going to Jamaica that week. We needed a vacation too. But still come! Someone will be happy to see you. Remember Royal? I see him every now and then. He comes by to do yard work and he asks about you a lot. He used to have a crush on you when y'all were kids. Go ahead and reconnect."

Not my mom trying to be a match maker. But little does she know, Royal and I have reconnected in the last couple of weeks. He already knows about me flying into town because he's my ride from the airport. Here's what I can say about Royal, when he messaged me it was a can he pursue me type of message. He wants to get to know his crush all over again. After dealing with Jabari, I swore off dealing with men and here comes Royal. Since I already knew him, I didn't look at him in a romantic way. But I'm not against seeing where things go if it goes anywhere.

After talking to my mom, I let Michelle know that I'm leaving in a couple weeks. "Don't fuck Royal." The look I had on my face as she walked away after saying that had me in shock. Why can't I have fun? I wasn't thinking about doing anything with him though. We haven't seen each other since we were kids. It'll just be a reunion even though he wants to see if I'm someone he would want in his life. As I'm walking to the kitchen to get some food, I receive a call from Royal. I let him know instantly that my parents are actually gonna be out of town while I'm there, so I'll be house sitting.

"Maybe we can step out a couple nights then. I can take you around the city. Show you a good time. I wanna see how much my crush has grown over the years. Just don't be boring, alright?" Royal said as he was laughing.

I let him know that I'm down for all the shenanigans. Whatever he has planned for us is fine with me. He's definitely not going to get hit with me being boring. Or shy. Or whatever he thinks I am. After we discussed my itinerary, we went right back into catching up on our lives. One thing I can say about Royal is when it comes to our talks, there's no judgement, you would think we were friends that talk all the time. I even told him about me being in rehab. He was surprised but he didn't judge me. Royal told me if I relapsed to call him, that he gives great advice. It's like he tapped into another side of me. I'm never this open.

As soon as I ended my phone call with Royal, my phone started vibrating again. I wanted to ignore it. Jabari's name popping up was unexpected. I decided to answer it. Before I could even get hello out, he jumped right into what he needed to say.

"Nomi I really don't understand why you had to ask if I was fucking anyone else. The way my dick was deep in that pussy and you worrying about if I'm fucking someone else? Now I get it, you started to catch feelings. Fuck!"

I cut Jabari off before he could say another word. I let him know that regardless if I caught feelings or not, there was no need to cut me off. I told him his actions spoke volumes and that was my sign to not let him back in. The way Jabari is trying to justify his actions is driving me insane. He could've told me that he wasn't feeling the same way or clarified what he wanted but instead he did a bitch move and left me alone. Now he wants to question me about catching feelings?! We were spending three to four days a week together.

I come over, he's cooking, we eat together, talk, cuddle up on the couch and watch a movie, then we head to the bedroom and fuck and fall asleep together. I'm not saying he doesn't have feelings, that this can just be naturally him. But don't play me like that isn't the most intimate thing we could be doing just as "friends". It takes me back to this one night when he told me he doesn't know why women fall for him. That he doesn't do anything but be himself. Being himself is the reason why I fell for him, I guess.

Going back and forth on the phone with Jabari was getting us nowhere and I told him this is the last time I'll give him any of my time. I already know the type of man he is. When he doesn't get his way or a female does him wrong, he blocks them. That's a bitch move but I know I'm probably blocked from the moment we hung up. Dick comes and goes. I know he was the first to break my celibacy but there will be more when I'm ready for that time to come. I can say I'm glad I didn't fall into his trap and kept going around for his benefit. Putting how I feel to the side is not an option.

Waking up this morning, my anxiety was through the roof. I'm seeing Royal today and after last night, I don't know how to feel or where we stand. The night keeps playing over in my head. Last night as I was about to get in the shower, Royal called me on facetime. I was wrapped in my towel and he kept telling me to go ahead and get in the shower but to give him a show. Since I enjoyed talking to him, I sat my phone up in the shower. He kept laughing telling me to stop teasing him until he saw me get in the shower.

The look on his face made me laugh. I decided to put on a show like he asked. When it came to washing myself, I washed my titties before playing with my nipples. When it came to washing my back, I turned around to let the soap wash off, bending over spreading my ass to let the water run down all the way to my feet. After having fun in the shower, I wanted to keep going.

Seeing Royal's reaction turned me on. This started off as laughs and giggles but the moment I saw his hand stroking his dick, I knew I had his attention. After the shower, I sat the phone on my vanity and began to dry myself off while standing in front of my tall mirror. Royal had a full view. I lotioned myself up and went back to sitting on the vanity where I took an oil made for clit and first rubbed it all on the hood of my pussy. I then started to spread my lips to show my clit and Royal's entire face was in the camera like he was about to lick it. Before he could even say anything, I started to play with my clit and rubbing my nipple at the same time. Royal kept stroking his dick every time I looked up to look at him. I felt myself about to cum and I let him know.

    I got myself together and the first thing Royal said was, "this was definitely unexpected, but I appreciate it." I couldn't do anything but laugh. How does he get this side of me to come out? Everything is flowing so natural, he just seems too good to be true. Coming out of rehab, I remember Dr. Johnson told me, "The person who gets you, is the one you won't expect. But that will happen once you're healed and take control of what you do with your body." Dr. Johnson always let it be known to love myself first and things will fall in place. I know I'm getting ahead of myself with Royal but I have this feeling about him that I can't shake.

    Michelle was busy so Nala took me to the airport. Since I haven't mentioned Jabari's name in awhile, she decided to ask me about him. I let her know he's no longer a problem because I don't deal with anymore. It's been two months since I've dealt with him. What's the saying, more dick in the sea? I'm not going back to the old me but I'm learning to live for me. I don't need multiple men to satisfy me. Nala mentioned Royal but I ignored her and asked how's couple's therapy was going. She gave me the side eye.

    She let me know that there is growth and her and Elijah are in a much better place. Which explains why she hasn't been around much. We always told her to stay home, it's okay to miss out. We all hardly get together as it is, unless it's someone's birthday or we plan an event. But each one of us has our own lives and takes care of ourselves first.

    Nala hugged me and told me to have fun and enjoy myself. She knows whenever I go back home it's nothing but a party. I wonder how it's going to go now with my parents being in Jamaica and the friends I did have, no longer live in Chicago. If Royal wants to entertain me the majority of the week then so be it.

The plane ride was smooth but felt like forever. I text Royal letting him know I landed. I grabbed my bag from the baggage claim and the moment I stepped outside, he was pulling up. The butterflies in my stomach started going crazy. Royal stepped out to help me with my bags then hugged me tightly.

"About time you made your way back to the windy city."

Hearing him speak on me like this, I have to remember I was a crush of his. Of course he is happy that I'm back visiting and the fact that he is the one picking me up makes it better. The ride to my parent's house was peaceful. Every time I look over at Royal, he's looking at me like he can't believe I'm actually here. When we got to the house, Royal tried staying in the car. I told to bring his ass inside. He had a day planned for us, but I wanted to shower and change first. He carried my bags to my room and got comfortable on my bed. I went through my bag to look for an outfit. Once I did that, it was time to tease him.

I started to strip and he looked at me like what the fuck am I doing. I started with my shirt, exposing my lace bra. Then my leggings came off, showing my lace thong. I stared at Royal in his eyes as I reached behind my back to unhook my bra, letting my titties show with my hard nipples. His eyes widened as I started to take my thong off. I turned around so he could watch this ass walk off to the bathroom. I looked back and noticed his dick was getting hard. I smiled walking away.

While in the shower my mind started to wonder. Would Dr. Johnson agree with what I'm doing? I feel like I'm going backwards. But then again, it's been almost three months since I've had sex. I cleared the thoughts out of my head and focused on the now. I have an attractive, fine as fuck man waiting on my bed that wants to fuck me.

Walking back into the room wrapped in my towel, Royal had music playing. He looked at me and told me that I'm beautiful and to stop teasing him. I sat on the bed and he got up. As Royal is walking out of the room, I stand up to dry myself. The moment I opened my towel, he turned around and came rushing towards me. His lips pressed against mine before his tongue entered my mouth. Royal laid me on the bed and got on top of me, kissing me some more. He started to kiss down my body. Once he got to my pussy, he asked me to spread my lips open. I did what he asked and the way he sucked my clit had me moaning instantly.

My clit was extremely sensitive to his tongue, I wasn't sure if I could take it. But it felt so good, my cries out made him go insane. The work of his tongue is like a paint brush working its way around my clit. Eating pussy is a form of art that he is exceptionally amazing at doing. My moans became louder as I reached the point of about to climax. When Royal noticed the difference in my breathing, he focused on making that climax happen. That orgasm is one for the books. When he sat up and looked at me, his beard was soaking in my juices, dripping off his face. I don't know what came over me but I pulled him in and kissed him like it was the last day on earth. He brought out a passionate side of me and I didn't care.

Royal had this touch to him as if he was learning my body while sexing me. He held my legs up, kissing them before inserting himself inside of me. This man was making love to my body but also my mind. I lifted my hips up to feel him go deeper inside of me. He put his hand on my neck and somehow managed to get me on top and him on his back. I got off his dick to turn myself around and reverse cowgirl on him. Holding his ankles, bouncing up and down on him, hearing him go crazy is turning me on. Royal's hands going up and down on my back before holding my waist to control the movement on his dick is a teaching moment. Yes baby, tell me how you would want me to work your dick.

Here he goes again, moving us like we're a rubrics cube. Royal leaned me all the way over to start beating the pussy up from the back. With my ass tooted up and him spreading my cheeks to get that full effect. The more he is stroking, I feel his dick growing more in me. I start to feel it throbbing and I begin to tighten my walls when he strokes. He lets me know he's about to cum and I continue to grip on his dick. As he's cumming, he lets out a loud growl and that shit turns me on. I almost wanted him to put his dick back in me. Until I realized that he never pulled out. Royal is laying on my back, dick still in me.

While I'm trying to get Royal's attention, he's telling me to relax, that the pussy feels too good to get out of. This man can't be serious. "Royal get off of me, let me clean off your dick." He looked at me confused but did as I said. Once he was on his back, his dick was down my throat tasting my juices. I'm surprised by how much I've creamed on his dick. With all the men I've been with, I only glaze the dick. I sucked Royal's dick until he climaxed. Tasting myself on his dick then tasting him seemed like a good mix in my mouth.

We laid in bed trying to figure out how we got to this point. Royal said watching me in the shower turned him on so he was going to fuck me. He didn't plan for it to happen on the first day in town though. I told him I didn't mind, that teasing him was going to lead to it anyway. "Never thought I would be fucking my crush. Plus getting to know you all over again is a bonus. You're wild but down to earth. I love our conversations. You have me on the phone for hours."

I was trying to focus on what Royal was saying but he's caressing my titty while talking to me so all I'm thinking about is round two. I stopped his hand and he moved it down to my thigh moving it open. He started to finger my pussy before playing with my clit. I looked him in his eyes and he took my nipple in his mouth. I started to grip the sheets and moan his name. I felt myself about to cum so quickly, I lifted his face off my nipple and started kissing him. But his hand on my clit was not stopping the sensitivity. Royal went back to my nipple and I lost it. I yelled I was cumming and he kept going. After my orgasm, he kept touching my clit and I was begging him to stop. That feeling is unexplainable. Royal kissed my cheek and finally stopped teasing me.

We got ourselves together and headed out. I was hungry as fuck. We pulled up to this Italian spot and I was okay with it. Can't go wrong with pasta. After eating I asked to go back home. I was overly exhausted from flying and fucking and now I have food on my stomach, I'm ready to pass out. Royal asked if it's fine that he stays the week with me. I actually would want him to stay. Something about being in a house by myself scares me when it's not my own. I gave Royal the okay. We stopped by his place first so he could grab his things. Once we got back to my parent's place, he checked all the doors and windows and made sure everything was locked up. By the time he was finished with that, I was naked in bed sound asleep. I woke up for a second when I felt him wrap his arms around me to cuddle while sleeping.

The next few days have been interesting. That's the only way I can describe it because I have been speechless when I think about it. Each morning, I've been woken up to his tongue fucking my pussy. When we step out, we're in the restaurant and he's fingering me under the table. While he's driving, I've leaned over and started sucking his dick. One night we pulled up to a park and fucked in the car. It was a lot of fucking going on that was not expected.

When my last day in town came, Royal asked if I ever thought about moving back to the city. He explained to me that spending this week with me has been one of the best times he's had in a long time. That I'm bringing out another side of him that he hasn't seen in a few years. Hearing him speak this way softens my heart. Sharing our stories, we had some similarities when it came to the dating world. He had so much love to give he wanted to find his person, after multiple failed relationships. I shut out the relationship side of me after two horribly failed relationships.

Part of me started to get concerned because after catching feelings for Jabari and that going sour, I wanted things with Royal to be sweet. Then I started thinking about the distance between us. How are we going to make this work? Until Royal asked me how I feel about California. He's looking into getting his master's degree in southern California. He'll be moving there next month. I can feel my face warming up and I'm trying not to be overly cute and excited. We've only been talking a little under a month and this week together was like a sign. I came with the intentions of whatever happens this week, just go with the flow. I let him get into my mind, he tapped into my pussy, and now my heart is slowly thawing out again.

While Royal was asleep, I contacted Dr. Johnson asking if I could set up an appointment. He thought it was an emergency and said I can come now. I let him know that I am out of town and will be back tomorrow. We made the appointment for the day after tomorrow. After hanging up with him, I turned around to Royal's eyes looking at me. "I like that you go to therapy, and get the help you need. Even if you feel like you're doing better than you were before, it doesn't hurt to get clarity."

I explained to Royal that I'm on the road to recovery. I'm not sure if the finish line is near or far away but I don't want to go back to the person I once was. It wasn't only about multiple sex partners and wild random sex with strangers. I had to dig deeper into my soul to find out why I was moving how I was moving. I pleased many men in regards to them wanting me and giving me a certain type of attention. I could have walked away, ignored them but it was my choice to entertain and fall through with it. The only time I can say it was up to me is when I made a starting five. Contacting the ones that actually satisfied me in different ways.

 Royal appreciated how open I was with him, I told him in a strange way, he was like my diary. He made it so easy to talk to him. We decided to not be so sentimental and enjoy my last day. We got ready and headed out the house. I mentioned that I was hungry and was wanting a deep dish from Giordano's. He rolled his eyes and tried to argue me down in regards to better pizza spots. But I had to remind him I don't get real deep dish pizza in Portland. He shut up and turned the music up.

 I had him acting like a tourist downtown Chicago and he wasn't having it but he didn't have a choice. After leaving Giordano's we walked to The Bean at Millennium Park and I made him take pictures with me. Then we walked down to the Chicago Theater, so I could get a picture in front of the sign. Royal already let me know his pet peeve is doing tourist things in the city so I made it my job to do just that. It was a testing moment. If he became overly upset by it then that will give me the answer I'm looking for. Surprisingly he was going with the flow of things while calling me a tourist. At least he's having fun with me.

When we got back home we both passed out. I woke up to him pleasing my pussy and sucking on my nipple. He was trying to get me aroused and once he did, his dick was slid right inside of me. He leaned in to make out with my neck before holding onto my titties as he stroked in and out of me. The way he moved his hips to make his dick curve perfectly in me had my mind running wild. Tell me you know your way around pussy without telling me you know your way around pussy. He held my legs up and spread them apart while fucking the shit out of me. My moans kept getting louder and I knew what was about to happen and so did Royal. He leaned down to whisper in my ear.

"Cum on this dick."

Hearing those words with him going deeper while now sucking on my nipple, had my eyes roll to the back of my head. I yelled I'm about to cum and he felt his dick soaking up from my orgasm which made him cum right after me. After he released himself inside of me, we laid there, hot and sweaty underneath the fan trying to cool down. Sex with him is definitely amazing. I fell asleep instantaneously.

I woke up to my alarm going off but Royal was already up. He was laying in bed playing with my curls. "I wish this week didn't come to an end. But I'll be seeing you soon anyway. I'll be in Cali next month, much closer to you. You're not going anywhere. And now I feel like I've said too much and let you into my mind."

Why did he have to hit me with this as soon as I opened my eyes? The butterflies in my stomach kept flying around. Now I really don't want to go back home. I told Royal he will see me when he gets settled and ready for me to come visit him. He pulled me in closer then told me to get ready. It is that time to head to the airport soon. I took a shower, got dressed then finished packing up my bag. I was so focused on getting my things together, I didn't realize Royal was standing behind me. I turned around and screamed, which made him laugh. He hugged me and said I'm cute when I'm scared.

"Let me get your bags and you make sure everything is good in the house. Don't need your parents coming back home complaining about something you forgot to do. Believe me, I won't hear the last of it."

I love that Royal helps my parents out with yard work or something done in the house. If we were to try to build something between us, I'd already have my parents' approval. He already has his replacement ready to step in when he moves next month. I couldn't be more grateful for all he does. After making sure the house is good, I locked up and we began to head to the airport. This was a much needed vacation and I'm glad that Royal came back into my life. It was unexpected but isn't that how most journeys begin?

Pulling up to the airport, I wanted to cry. I wasn't ready to go back home. It sucks, but it's time to return to reality. Looking at my phone, I noticed I wasn't responding to anyone. I just now decided to text Michelle letting her know what time I'll be landing. Royal got out of the car to grab my bags and open my door. Stepping out of the car I pulled him in for a hug. I thanked him for a great week and he kissed my forehead while telling me he's happy I still decided to come out with my parents not being in town. I laid my head on his chest before pulling away. Walking into the airport, I turn around and he's watching me. I smiled and waved before walking away. I think I'm actually going to miss him.

Sitting in Dr. Johnson's office once again is making me feel a little relaxed. My anxiety isn't flaring. I'm calm. I can't wait to see him and tell him about my trip. I feel like he's going to have something to say against it but maybe if I tell him how it made me feel, he might be supportive and shocked but grateful for my growth. Dr. Johnson walks in and has a seat. He greets me and mentions how he's glad that I still decide to have our sessions if needed.

"Okay Nomi, last time you were here, you mentioned that you broke your celibacy and enjoyed this man's company. How are things going with you two?"

I explained that things are over between Jabari and I. I told him that I asked Jabari a simple question if he was fucking other women. He told me at first he was but then it was just me. For some reason, with me asking him that, it made him feel uncomfortable because he cut me off right after that. Dr. Johnson's face once again makes me laugh. He never knows what's going to come out of my mouth. But I continued on to tell him that I went two months without any intimacy. I told him about Royal. I explained that Royal is a friend from childhood, he actually had a crush on me as kids. When my parents moved back home to Chicago my dad was doing the yardwork. When Royal came back to Chicago after graduating college, he started to help my parents out.

Dr. Johnson liked that Royal was helpful to my parents but wanted to know more about why I'm really mentioning him. I told him that Royal reached out to me in wanting to pursue me. Get to know me all over again. I told him that my parents went out of town so Royal kept me entertained. I mentioned that we did have sex, every single day. But the difference with him from Jabari and all the other men I dealt with, Royal actually made love to my mind while touching my body. I wanted him to touch me. If another man wants to touch me, I don't think I can let that happen. He did something no other man has ever done. It changed something in me.

Royal learned my body the way I know my body when I please myself. He knows my mind the way I know my mind. He points out things about myself that I didn't even think anyone could see. I told Dr. Johnson that I told Royal about me being here in rehab, he also knows about today's therapy session. He supports it. Now as I'm telling him this, I also let it be known that I can recognize when a man is trying to run a game on me and Royal is not doing that at all. Everything about him is genuine.

"From my understanding, with all the men you dealt with, you looked for sexual satisfaction only. You guarded your heart that you never let anyone in to even get to know you if they tried. Now an old friend from childhood comes back around in your life and things are different for you. And I believe because he is good with your parents and helps them out, gives you a different outlook on him. I'm not saying be careful but don't be quick to let your guard down. But I am proud of how far you've come. From the woman that came to this facility unsure about being here to taking control and thinking things through. You're learning more about yourself and realizing things that you didn't catch onto before."

Tears started to flow and I couldn't control them. I haven't had anyone tell me how they notice my growth. That I'm not that woman that I once was. Hearing Dr. Johnson speak those words made me proud of myself. I kept questioning if I was doing something wrong when my friends kept making sure I didn't go back to how I was. They really didn't encourage the change, only reminded me of what I normally don't do. I thanked Dr. Johnson for acknowledging my efforts. I really needed to hear it. My session has come to an end and before stepping out the office, I hugged Dr. Johnson and thanked him again.

I sat in the parking lot to get myself together before driving off. I received a facetime call from Royal and answered it without even checking if I was good. The first thing he said was that my therapy session had to be an emotional one because my eyes are kind of red as if I've been crying. I told him all about it and he even said I should be proud of myself. I started to cry again but I told him it was happy tears. My friends treat me like I'm going back to that life. No one has faith in me but I have to have faith in knowing that I'm always going to move forward. I have to be my own inspiration and motivation.

Talking to Royal made my day better. He's very understanding and he listens to me. Sometimes that's all I want is a listening ear. He filled me in on his move to California. He's all set and has a place secured too. Royal also asked if I can fly out the day he gets in town. He wants to bless his place with my pussy. This man is so nasty, I love it. I told him once he gets the date squared away, then I'll get my ticket.

I told him that I need to get busy and I'll talk to him later on. We hung up and I went on about my day.

Over the next few weeks, life has been busy nonstop. I feel like someone has put an ad out for me with my photography because I have appointments set up everyday. I had to add a block week on my scheduling because I'm going to Cali. Between my regular job, my side hustle, and these crazy dreams I've been having, everything else has been sane surprisingly. Each one of my girls have been occupied. I hardly see Michelle because she's always at Lawrence's place. I've had the house to myself and the quietness is peaceful. Royal and I have been growing stronger everyday. I can't wait to be around him again. I need his presence but I'll be patient.

One day after a long day of working both jobs, I came home and couldn't even make it up the stairs. I sat on the couch and called Royal. By the sound of my voice he told me to go to sleep. I was trying to tell him about this dream I used to have when I was in rehab, that started to circulate back again and it's been a daily dream for the past week. He told me we can talk about it tomorrow and to go to sleep. I don't even remember hanging up, I just know my mind drifted right into a deep sleep and right into my dream.

"Damn I never realized how attractive this cashier is. Has he always been this way or I just never paid him any attention?" I thought to myself as I'm waiting for him to ring up all my items. I look at his name tag, and see that his name is David. Now David is a little too skinny for my liking but that's okay his dark skin tone makes up for it and that amazing smile. I wonder if he's working with something to get this ocean flowing between my legs. Maybe he likes it rough, choke me, pull my hair type of man. Or he can be the soft, passionate love making caress your face type, kissing you while slowly stroking you missionary style. Let me get out of this Walgreens, before I jump over this counter.

It's been 150 days without the passion of dick beating me up proudly from the back, doggystyle, and I don't know what to do with myself. Every little touch or stare sends my mind on a run and won't stop until I'm laid on my back with my vibrator pleasuring me until I give myself the hundredth orgasm.

I wasn't always like this, I used to be that girl that would be the cause of the bathroom lines in the clubs being extra long because I'm drunk sucking some random's dick or being fucked. My friends know me as the wild one so when I hear, "Damn Nomi, you have changed. Lowkey miss getting your text about going out drinking and going home with someone." Now I'm making love to one of my many vibrators. One night it can be the rabbit, then the clitoris stimulator, or one of my favorites when I'm extremely horny is my thrusting vibrator that does it on its own.

I enjoy that I slowed down but have you ever been bumped on accident and the person apologizes to you and your response is, "No, thank you". Then you're finding a way for them to bump into you again because that's the most someone else has touched you in awhile. My number one love language is physical touch so it's crazy I'm punishing myself like this. I need hands caressing my breast and cuffing my ass then slowly going to my pussy to begin fingering it while using the other hand to continue to rub on my body. I find myself lost deep in my thoughts squeezing my breast staring off into space.

When that happens, I'm usually thinking to myself of what type of dick I want penetrating me. I would usually think about a thick long dick, well above average satisfying me but not this time. I want that uncircumcised dick inside of me. The way I can feel it growing with each stroke getting harder amazes me and gets me turned on even more. That extra skin isn't so bad after all. I also start to think about how sucking it will feel, growing in my mouth from getting hard but it's been so long since without dick, I think of things I can do to keep the man happy. Having his balls going in and out of my mouth while stroking his dick has me thinking about doing this to the next man I let break this cycle.

Alright Nomi, calm down, can't get yourself all excited for something you're not going to receive anytime soon.

I have to give myself pep talks before I flirt with

someone so hard I will end up in the back of their car riding that dick like it's the last one on earth. Let me grab the thrusting vibrator and get this orgasm over with. Rubbing the lube on the vibrator, my mind is already picturing this vibrator is a real dick I'm about to fuck. With my crazy nasty imagination, I don't even need a sex playlist to get me going, I'm already wet and dripping.

As I moan uncontrollably, I feel my phone vibrating but whoever is calling me is going to have to wait because I'm not stopping myself. Until I notice the vibration of my phone isn't stopping, but my dick vibrator has stopped! I instantly start screaming out of anger."

When I woke up, I quickly called Royal. Before he could get hello out, I started to talk about my dream. He mentioned maybe its coming back around because this around the time you checked yourself into rehab to get better. It's a memory of your mind that reminded you how you were coping with celibacy. He also said it's no point of me getting so worked up over it. That I need to just breathe. Royal reassured me that everything is going to be fine. And he told me to remember how far I've come to look at my progress. "Now please go back to sleep, it's seven in the morning here which makes it five out there. I'll talk to you at a decent hour." I told him goodnight and went back to sleep.

The first thing I did when I woke up was grab my journal. One thing Dr. Johnson suggested that I do is write things out. It's part of being on the road to recovery. I wrote out all my feelings, fears, and goals. I'll never forget the person I was. But as Royal and Dr. Johnson pointed out, I should be proud of my growth. I move carefully when it comes to certain things. When it comes to myself, I'll always put myself first. After writing my entry for the day, I hit the group chat to see about having a girls night. We've all been so busy, I miss them. Everyone must've been thinking the same because they all responded back saying yes. Michelle must still be asleep, only one that didn't respond.

Walking downstairs to get myself something to eat, I screamed at the top of my lungs. My view was unexpected. Michelle and Lawrence was butt ass naked fucking on the couch. When I screamed, Lawrence turned towards me and I went back to my room. Fifteen minutes passed before Michelle knocked on my door. She came in and I'm laughing because this has never happened. "Before you say anything, we were in my room. I was getting ready to walk him out but when he kissed me goodbye, the kiss turned into more as you saw." I guess it was my payback because years ago Michelle caught me having sex with someone on her couch. When we walked back downstairs, Lawrence was still there. Michelle walked to the kitchen and left me alone with Lawrence. I just got set up now.

"I'm sure you know why I want to talk to you. Besides the fact that you saw all my business. But you remember my cousin Jabari right? He told me how things went down and I feel as if it's my part because I told you to be careful. Did my comment cloud your head that much? Or were you already catching feelings when I said it?"

I told Lawrence that his comment did make me think but I didn't know it was going to cause Jabari to cut me loose. I let him know that he tried to come back but went about it in an asshole way by only speaking on the way he was fucking me. Lawrence put his head down in disappointment. He apologized on his cousin's behalf. I didn't want to hear it. It is what it is. I let him know I'm not even worried about him. I've moved on and I'm glad I did. I told Lawrence no more trying to attempt matchmaking and hugged him goodbye.

Right when the front door closed, Michelle came walking out the kitchen like nothing happened. I gave her the side eye because she should have said something. Michelle reassured me that when Lawrence asked her about speaking to me about Jabari, she was against it. But he said he just wanted to ask me about it, not get too deep into it. Since I'm over the whole situation, I wish everyone else would get over it. I changed the subject and asked Michelle if she was down for a girls night.

"Girl while you were talking to Lawrence and I responded in the group chat, Ashley, Renee, and Tiana said they forgot they had plans."

We can't ever get together. And next week I'm going to Cali so no one's schedule is aligned at the moment. Maybe when I get back we can do something. Nala asked if she and Zuri could come over today and hang out with us. It's been awhile since I've seen them so we said sure. I told Michelle we need to spray down this couch because it's contaminated with her sex juices. She rolled her eyes then got annoyed when I pulled the spray out already. My goddaughter is about to come over and she always falls asleep on this couch so it's time to clean up.

Nala wasted no time as soon as she came through the door. She wanted to know about Royal and Chicago and whatever else I missed out on. "So I walked in on Michelle and Lawrence fucking on the couch. His ass was out and she was just completely naked. Come to think of it, you said you were walking him out? I think you were actually out here getting it on because why did you have to strip all the way down? Anyways that's whatever else you missed out on."

Michelle gave me a glare and Nala told Zuri to stay off the couch. I laughed and ended up giving them both the spill on Royal. Once I mentioned that he knows about me going to rehab and my crazy sex stories, their eyes became wide. I explained that I felt comfortable telling him. We were playing this game of who has done worse things and that's how my rehab came up. He didn't judge me for what I went through. Royal gave great advice and he listened.

Hearing how Royal was encouraging made Nala and Michelle feel a type of way. They realized that they were too busy trying to make sure I don't turn back into a wild one instead of telling me how proud they should be of me this past year. I lived in fear for six months after I left rehab and none of my friends encouraged me to step out. I'm not saying it's their job but I had to motivate myself and I'm glad that I found myself and pushed myself to get out of fear.

My girls hugged me and apologized. I didn't

hold anything against them but I told them it's not too late to keep me on the right path. I'm not saying in regards to having my therapist and Royal on my side. I just want people who have known me for years to show some faith. After a sentimental moment, I ended up telling them about going to California with Royal. I told them he's moving there and he wants me to come out when he gets in. They quickly started making kissing sounds and even Zuri came out of nowhere singing the kissing song. All we heard was "K-I-S-S-I-NG". We couldn't do anything but laugh.

  This day was much needed. Starting off funny then some tears came along and back to showing love and expressing our growth. It's not the whole gang but it's still better than spending the day alone. While the night was coming to an end, Nala said her and Zuri should be heading out. She needed to take Nala to her mom's house because she and Elijah are having a date night. I'm happy they turned their marriage around. The love they share is strong and they can work it out through anything. As they were leaving, Lawrence called Michelle wanting to see if she wanted to come over. She told him it's a girls night and he respected it. I told her she can go, but she can tell I've been missing her because she's never home anymore. So she stayed and we did our hair and nails like we used to as kids when we used to have sleepovers.

Why do our nights always end with us munching on a bunch of snacks and a large pizza? Michelle is a smoker but I smoke with her on occasions and this is how I get. The munchies are real! Royal was calling me on facetime and I got excited. Right when I answered, Michelle grabbed the phone and had to introduce herself as my bestie and the only one I will have. He hit her with, "Well I don't know about that, Nomi talks to me like I'm her diary, so I think that beats out your spot."

Now why did Royal have to say that? Michelle looked at me and yelled "Diary?!". To avoid this going any further I told Michelle that Royal has a dick. She shut up real quick and passed me my phone. Royal laughed and I told him he ain't have to show out like that. Of course he likes to have fun. He told me that he can't wait to see me next week. I can't lie, I miss his company. Another week spent with Royal is ahead of me and I'm excited. It's been awhile since I've been to Southern Cali, and the fact that he's never been to the state is going to be fun to experience with him.

When our call ended, Michelle pokes her head around the corner and has to point out how cute we are. The butterflies in my stomach always appear when I hear his name or speak to him. I explained that feeling to her and once again she hit me with the "awww so cute!". I'm sick of her but it makes me feel all mushy inside. Plus the way he makes my pussy feel. I can't get over the fact that he makes love to my body so fucking good. His touch is sensational. Thinking about it gives me chills. Let's see what next week brings us.

I forgot how busy LAX airport is and my anxiety is starting to flare. I made my flight come in around the same time as Royal's but if it was up to me, I would have taken the last flight out. I'm glad we both flew in on Southwest so I told Royal what gate I'm flying into. Our gates were ten gates apart but it took forever to get to him. When I finally made it to Royal, I walked right up to him with open arms. I was aiming for a hug but he had other things in mind when he greeted me with a passionate kiss. I felt my nipples get hard and my pussy beginning to drip along with the chills all over my body. When we pulled away, I was ready to jump on his dick. I had to remember where I was.

We made it to baggage claim to grab our bags and make our way to the uber. The moment we got in our uber, I looked at the driver's phone and it said forty-five minutes. Fuck this traffic, damn! I thought about how Royal made me feel in the airport and I thought about returning the favor. I laid on his lap and started rubbing his dick. I looked up at him and he looked at me like I don't have the balls to do it. Say less! I pulled my hoodie over my head and took his dick out of his sweats. Without question, I took it right in my mouth. As he started getting hard, I went deeper.

"Fuck Nomi, this how you get down. Fuck."

Royal was trying to talk low so the uber driver wouldn't hear us. Good thing he was on the phone. Royal put his hand on my head to help me go deeper. I took his dick out my mouth and started kissing the outside of it while massaging his balls. His moans were quiet but hearing him whisper fuck many times made please him more. I put his balls and my mouth while stroking his dick.

Royal told me to go easy on his balls. I have to remember they're sensitive. I took his dick back in my mouth and started to deep throat again but this time, I kept going deeper and he told me to keep going just like that. Royal said he's about to cum and I felt it coming. Once he released, I swallowed all of him and kept going until he begged me to stop.

I tucked his dick back in his sweats and laid on it like it was the best pillow I've had. Royal sat me up and wanted to return the favor back to me. He laid in-between my legs, face planted in my pussy. Royal told me to cover his head up with my hoodie. Was this man really about to eat my pussy in this uber?! Before I knew it, he had my leggings down and tongue right on my clit. He held my pussy lips open to go deeper. It took everything in me not to moan loudly. I feel like I want to take the risk and give a show. I let out a quiet but noticeable moan and I saw the driver look in his rearview mirror.

Royal had to forgetten that we were in the uber because there's no way he is tongue fucking my pussy like this. My moans are growing louder and I see the driver more interested. I noticed his left hand was on his lap and when he looked back in the mirror, I winked at him. I can tell that made him nervous because he put both hands back on the wheel. I felt myself about to cum and I know Royal felt it too because his tongue started going wild. I covered my mouth as I was cumming but the driver still noticed because my breathing changed. The driver's face was in shock.

As Royal is licking up the last of my juices, I tried to move away from him while laughing, begging him to stop. I felt him pull my leggings up and he continued to lay on my lap the rest of the ride. When we pulled up to Royal's new apartment, the driver quickly hopped out to help me out of the car and even offered to carry my bags but Royal shut that down. He let him know that he got it from here and thanked him for the ride. As we started walking to his place, I let him know that the driver was enjoying a little show during the ride. I told him it was hard for me to control my face. We laughed about it and he was not expecting me to go along with it.

Royal opened the door to his place and I was surprised. It was fully furnished. From the living room, to the kitchen, bathroom and bedrooms. I asked him when and how this happened. He told me that he has a cousin that stays out here and helped him get everything together. I was impressed how he takes care of business. While he was getting himself situated, I stepped out onto the balcony. I took in the air and was happy to be on another vacation. The only difference this time is, it's not a vacation for Royal. This is his new home and come next week, he'll be starting on his master's program at USC.

I felt Royal hands wrapping around me, hugging me tight from behind. He told me that he can get use to this, that it feels like we haven't been apart for a month. Royal started to kiss the side of my neck before whispering in my ear asking if I like an audience. I nodded yes and he reached into my leggings and was happy to see that I'm still wet. He slowly pulled my leggings down while giving a kiss on my ass. His view from his balcony is the city and at this moment the sun was beginning to set. Royal fucking me outside felt like it was only us in the world. If people were watching, I didn't feel them. The way he works my mind, I'm not thinking about anything except for how good he is making me feel.

I was so far gone in a different world with the way he is fucking me, I didn't realize that he pulled his dick out until I felt fingers in my pussy and a tongue in my ass. I'm starting to see that ass eating is becoming more of a thing in my life. He's the third one to do this to me. Yet again here he goes treating my body like it's art. I didn't know you could make eating ass feel like you're floating. He took his fingers out my pussy and spread my cheeks to stick his tongue further in me. My moans became too much. Royal quickly stopped and told me to go to the bedroom.

When I entered the bedroom, I took a peek in the bathroom. It was huge! Double sinks with a tub with jets and the shower next to it. The shower had a spot where you can sit and my mind went to my next idea. While Royal was making sure everything was good before coming into the bedroom, I shut the bathroom door and started the shower. I took off my clothes and got in. I heard Royal calling my name. After a few minutes, he finally decided to check the bathroom and I couldn't do anything but laugh.

Royal opened the shower door, with his dick hard as a rock. I told him to have a seat. He walked into the shower and stood under the shower head to kiss me first before sitting down. I walked over to him and sat right on the dick and began to bounce on it. Royal took my titty in his mouth and started sucking on my nipple while holding onto my hips. He started to work his hips and pump that dick in me harder and I started to lose control as I felt myself about to cum.

This orgasm is more intense than usual. When I came, I almost fainted. Royal caught me and held me. I stood up and he stepped out for a second to grab some soap and towels. Royal washed me up and once I was rinsed off, he told me to go to bed. I did as he said. I tried to wait on him, but I was asleep in less than five minutes being in the bed.

Waking up the next morning, feeling Royal arms wrapped around me took me back to the first time we laid in bed together. I thought about what he said, getting use to being around one another. It's nice, I like it. If someone was to ask me a year ago could I see myself traveling with a man, my answer would be no. I was too busy with a roster, being a hoe. Not catching feelings at all. Only sleeping around and leaving it at that. I never stayed the night at anyone's house. The first time I did that was with Jabari. That ended after a couple months. Then Royal. I could've canceled my trip to Chicago since my parents weren't there but I still went and had a great time. Now I'm in California with him, in his new home.

Is this how life is supposed to go after rehab? I mean this is a record for me. Two men in one year. I can say I'm proud of myself. I had more hit me up but they were old bodies and I didn't want to go backwards. And it's happening again, my feelings are getting involved. But this is different. Royal got to know my mind first, then got my pussy but even while getting the pussy, he got to know my body. I can't get over how his touch makes me feel. I can't describe it but I know I want more of it.

When I turned around to look at Royal he was already looking at me. He said I looked like I was deep in thought so he didn't want to disturb me. I told him how I was thinking about my life and how much I've changed. "I'm sure the old you wasn't that bad. If you had someone worth your time, you could have stopped dealing with all these men to focus on that one. I'm not saying this in regards to rehab wasn't necessary. You did what was best for you and it helped. You got to tell your story to a complete stranger and that's bold enough. You locked yourself away for three months. You had to find answers within yourself and with help from what it sounds like, a great therapist."

Royal is that person that I need in my life. He's more than a want. Even if he's just a friend, I'm okay with that. I have no clue where things are going with us but I'm happy to feel included in the changes in his life. He didn't have to ask me to come here and experience his first week here but he did. I didn't have to tell him about my wild stories, but when he dished it back with his stories, I felt comfortable. Not even my closest friends know everything that I've done. I mentioned the random worker from the hotel to him and he told me he fucked a random woman in the parking lot of Target. He made me feel like my decisions in life weren't so bad. He wanted me to live life, to be free.

Over the next few days, we explored the city. We tried different foods so he can get an idea of what he'll enjoy that's in the area. I had him do one tourist thing for me, which was to go to The Dunes, the apartment building that's featured on my favorite show Insecure. The annoyance in his face will always make me laugh. One thing I was excited about was visiting USC. Royal wanted to get a feel of campus and this was a perfect time to do it. He had a quick orientation to do, so I walked around the campus seeing what all they have to offer. I saw a student with a camera and walked right up to them. I asked if there is a photography major here. She told me it's a photography minor that I can take and pointed me towards the art building.

I was amazed at the work I saw. My skills are on this level but I can use some improvements. Maybe I can take a few photography classes when I get back home to work on my skills. I don't need to spend unnecessary money for tuition. Royal's orientation must be over because he's calling asking where I am. I met him in the center of campus and his face lit up. Seeing his excitement made me proud of him. Not everyone can up and move their life for their goals. Many people will be too comfortable and scared of change. Not Royal, he goes after what he wants in life.

After leaving USC, we took an uber to the Toyota dealership. I became annoyed, not with him but at the fact that here goes hours of being stuck at the dealership while dealing with the process of getting a car. When we made it to our destination, we walked into the building and he asked me to wait here, he won't be long. Royal so far has had things taken care of in regards to his place and school. If he got a car already lined up and we are out of here in twenty minutes, I'll be impressed. Royal walked up to me and said for us to walk outside. In the next few minutes, an all black Camry pulled up in front of us. The dealer handed Royal the keys and opened the door for me and told us to have a good day.

"Lord, if you sent me this man to help turn my life around and show me everything different from what I've come across, thank you!"

There is no way Royal can be this amazing. I'm in shock but I don't want to show it too much. Nowhere in my mind was I ever doubting him, but the way he moves makes my pussy wet. I caressed his beard as he was driving. I looked up at the car and noticed the panoramic sunroof and fell in love. I didn't notice that we made it back to his place until he jokingly told me to get out. I looked at him crazy and laughed because I wanted to stay in the car. He came around the car and opened my door.

"I'm sure I surprised you today. I like to plan things out and have everything in order. I was not going to be stranded in a whole new city. I had my place set up and furnished as you can see. School was already picked and taken care of. And I handled the car situation last night when you passed out after amazing shower sex."

I told him lets go inside. Once inside I told him to sit on the couch. I touched his dick and he was already semi-hard. He stopped me and wanted to please me instead. Royal picked me up and carried me to the bedroom. I want to marry this man. The way I'm in his arms I feel protected, safe. He laid me on the bed and started to unbutton my jeans. Royal pulled both my jeans and panties off at the same time. He pushed his face in my pussy and went crazy. Either I'm still sensitive from last night or something because I already feel an orgasm about to happen. I yelled I was about to cum within ten minutes of him licking me up and his tongue started flicking faster than usual.

After that orgasm, I was weak but that didn't stop him from turning me on my stomach and fucking from behind. The way his hands were pierced on my back, pulling me back on him as he's rocking my body on his dick had me ready to have another orgasm. I felt it about to happen and he was about to come also as I can feel his dick throbbing inside of me. We climaxed at the same time and both our bodies dropped on the bed. We both had to catch our breath, and after we were stable, sleep came upon us. All I remember is him receiving a knock on the door of a doordash order and it was Jersey Mike's. We ate and went back to sleep.

Today was my last day with Royal. While he was in the shower, I called Dr. Johnson to set up an appointment for tomorrow. After setting that up, Royal stepped back into the bedroom, I leaned my head forward expecting my forehead kiss that he likes to give me. But this time he switched it up, he lifted my head up to kiss me on my lips. It was the most passionate kiss I've ever had. Plus I'm not a kisser. Everything Royal does relaxes my soul and makes my pussy drip.

"Nomi, my time spent with you has me thinking about all types of things. I can't shake this feeling I have for you. I know I want more from you, I want all of you. You motivate me. Inspire me. I do things for myself. Never for a woman. It's something about you that makes me want to provide and I want to be that for you. You took steps in life that no woman will admit and I admire that about you. You own up to your shit. And that's attractive. Nomi, will you be my woman?"

I was speechless and didn't know what to say. Did Royal just ask me to be his?! This was not how I expected this trip to go at all. The butterflies in my stomach are more active. It feels like if I open my mouth they're all going to fly out. When I think about Royal, he reminds me of the "dream guy" I used to say I wanted when I lost my virginity. But after each failed attempt and only wanting sex from men, I lost wanting and needing my person. I had settled for the wild life and that only brought me loneliness at night. Now I know my true worth and I'm ready to take this chance with Royal.

"Royal, yes I'll be yours."

He hugged me so tight and started making out with me. The smile on his face was real and genuine. I've never seen this man smile so hard. I laid my head on his chest and everything felt right. When he looked at the time, I heard sadness in his voice when he said it's time to go. I reminded him that my job is remote and if he ever wants me to fly out, I'll be here. He whispered something and I asked for him to speak up.

"Or you can move here, be with me. Think about it."

And he's done it again! Can he stop making me speechless?! I told him I'll think about it and that surprised me. Thinking about moving my life and starting over? We'll see how I feel after being away from him for a week, then I'll decide. Maybe that's too soon, probably a month will be enough to make my decision. That gives him time to enjoy his space before I crowd it. I sat up to grab the rest of my things so we could head to the airport.

Heading to the airport, the car was silent. Royal rested his hand on my thigh and I rubbed the back of his head. He broke the silence by saying he's going to miss waking up to me, mainly miss staring at me while I'm asleep. He mentioned how he's happy that I said yes to being his. I wouldn't have it any other way. Pulling up to LAX is about to make me cry. Another great week spent with Royal but many more to come. We hugged for what felt like eternity. We kissed another passionate kiss, before he sucked my bottom lip before pulling away.

"When I get my classes figured out, and a balanced schedule, I'm going to have you back out here. Even though I believe the next time you come back will be your last time leaving. No pressure at all, I have to have my fun with you. No rush, as long as you're mine, we will work through it."

I let Royal know that when I decide to come back it'll be a surprise. With me saying that, it reminded him to give me something. He reached into his pocket and pulled out a key. Royal gave me a key to his place with a fingers crossed keychain! I almost want to say fuck going back home and staying here. I can buy new things. Or have Michelle ship my things. I almost want to tell him that I love him. I accepted the key and kissed him again. Just like last time he watched me until he couldn't see me.

Another session in Dr. Johnson's office. I was excited to be here. It's been over a year of coming to rehab, being here, leaving, dealing with my fears and much more. Everyday I'm proud of myself and I can't wait to express it all to Dr. Johnson. When he walked into his office, I had a big smile on my face. I told him I can't wait to start this session. He started off with his usual of asking me to fill him in on what's going on in my life. He also acknowledged my smile and said it looks good on me.

I told Dr. Johnson about going to Cali with Royal and spending a week with him while he gets settled into his new life. I mentioned how he had everything together. How I expected his place to not be completely furnished but it was, and he even got a brand new car. I told him how we went to USC so Royal could attend his orientation. I spoke on how it motivated me to get a minor in photography. Now here's the news that will make Dr. Johnson give me his shocked look.

"So listen to this, the reason I'm so happy is because Royal asked me to be his woman. I said yes I'll be his. Then we got to the airport and he gave me a key to his place because I said next time I visit him, I'm going to surprise him. I completely skipped over a major part! Royal asked me to move in with him! In my mind my answer is yes but I haven't told him yet. It's definitely something to think about but the way he makes me feel Dr. Johnson is unexplainable. Do you remember when you told me that everything I'm doing with multiple men can be saved for one? Well Royal is that one. He's the one that I've been needing in my life. And I'm so happy when it comes to him."

Dr. Johnson actually had a smile on his face. He told me he was happy for me. That I deserved all that was coming my way. He made sure that I knew my worth. That's all he was trying to tell me during our sessions while I was in here for three months. He told me while I was on the road of changes, it won't hurt to make another change.

"You mentioned to me that you were supposed to leave Portland after high school. But because you got accepted to PSU, you stayed. And your parents still left you. Don't miss out on your opportunity now. From everything you mentioned about Royal, the man has a good head on his shoulders and he's about handling business. And making sure he's good and now you're a part of him and he will look after you."

I'm tired of crying in front of Dr. Johnson but this is the first time the tears are happy tears. Everything he said, I understood. He spoke the truth to me and I appreciated it. I always have this flashback from the first time I stood in front of the doors to enter this building. I was lost and didn't know what to do with myself. Then the day I left this building, I sat in my car scared to get back to the outside world, but Dr. Johnson gave me words of encouragement. For six months after rehab I lived in fear. I put myself back in the world from under a rock and met someone. Jabari was like a trail run that prepared me for Royal. I'm actually glad Jabari fucked up because now I have my man.

Dr. Johnson said if I ever decided to move, and I still need his assistance, zoom calls will always be available for me. My session came to an end and he hugged me and told me he is beyond proud of me, to never forget how I started this journey, but to always look forward. I appreciated everything he has done for me. And I'll never forget all that I learned from him. I was thankful and lucky he is my therapist. There's a reason it was him and no one else.

Walking out of the facility to my car, I turned around and took it all in. Everything happens for a reason. I sat in my car and smiled looking in the rearview mirror. Leaving here is overly peaceful this time. I grabbed my phone and called Royal. He answered the phone by saying hello beautiful. There goes those butterflies flapping around in my stomach again.

"Hey baby, so I was thinking, and my answer is yes. Next month is my moving date. Can't wait to start this journey with you."

I would like to acknowledge the patience you all had while waiting on this book to be complete. Encouraging me, being excited for me, asking me about it. Doing all those things kept me going and I'm beyond thankful for all of you. So thank you again and you're greatly appreciated! Let's keep them coming!

Made in the USA
Columbia, SC
12 January 2025